I've travelled the world twice over,
Met the famous: saints and sinners,
Poets and artists, kings and queens,
Old stars and hopeful beginners,
I've been where no-one's been before,
Learned secrets from writers and cooks
All with one library ticket
To the wonderful world of books.

© JANICE JAMES.

THE NET

He was caught good and tight, with nowhere to run . . . A crooked fight manager, a doublecrossing dame, a power-mad waterfront boss and a murderer who killed with no rhyme or reason . . . between them, they had trapped him in a spot where the police were two steps behind him — and death was one step ahead.

Books by Edward S. Aarons
in the Ulverscroft Large Print Series:

ASSIGNMENT MALTESE MAIDEN

EDWARD S. AARONS

◆

THE NET

Complete and Unabridged

ULVERSCROFT
Leicester

First published in the
United States of America

First Large Print Edition
published November 1994

British Library CIP Data

Aarons, Edward S.
    The net.—Large print ed.—
Ulverscroft large print series: mystery
I. Title
813.54 [F]

ISBN 0–7089–3179–0

Published by
F. A. Thorpe (Publishing) Ltd.
Anstey, Leicestershire
Set by Words & Graphics Ltd.
Anstey, Leicestershire
Printed and bound in Great Britain by
T. J. Press (Padstow) Ltd., Padstow, Cornwall

This book is printed on acid-free paper

1

BARNEY lay in his bunk in the crew's quarters forward, feeling the easy rise and fall of the fishing schooner, his eyes fixed on the dim lamp that swung in its gimbals. Now and then he heard the quick, worried hoot of the *Mary Hammond*'s horn. Subconsciously he waited for it, braced against the repetitious irritation of the sound.

The fog had covered the fishing banks for three days, practically since they cleared Easterly Breakwater. It was a cold fog, smelling of the Labrador current and the late September chill that slipped down the New England coast. He could almost taste the ice in it. It crept in everywhere, shrouding the schooner, seeping in under the hatches and down the fo'castle ladder until there was a halo around the oil lamp and nothing seemed dry or warm. He hated it. He told himself for the thousandth time that he was a fool to answer Henry's letter and come back

1

to Easterly and a bigger fool to try to make amends to Henry by taking this trip with him.

The tiers of rough bunks were all empty except Barney's. The *Mary Hammond*, three days out of Easterly, plowed slowly across the tidal current forty miles from home, her gallows trembling with the weight of her drag as she fished the bottom. Henry ignored the fog, of course, intent on the harvest he was reaping. Barney sighed and tried to adjust his length to the crude sleeping quarters Henry had assigned him. It was just like Henry to make him bunk up forward like this. Not that he minded it so much. He had fished for shares on smaller and rougher boats than the *Mary Hammond*, but still, a man would think his own brother would have him bunk in with him in the skipper's quarters.

"To hell with it," Barney said aloud.

Someone came down the ladder from the deck and he saw it was Pedro DeFalgia, one of the two Portugee brothers. He'd known Pedro and Carlos ever since childhood and the two old men had tried their best to make him a fisherman. As Pedro came nearer Barney said: "Hey, amigo."

"Senhor Barney," the old man nodded. "You are awake?"

"Sure, Pedro."

The old man took off his red woolen cap and stood with his head cocked as if listening to the strain on the winch from the tow wires up above. He was a squat, chunky man with thick, curly gray hair and the sturdy build of an Azores fisherman. His weathered face looked troubled. He squinted in the light of the lamp, searching the tiers of wooden bunks. When he saw they were all empty except Barney's, he relaxed a little.

"You are alone?" he asked.

"Sure," Barney said again.

He swung his legs out of the bunk and sat up. He looked out of place in the rude quarters of the fishing schooner. His suede jacket and Fifth Avenue slacks didn't belong among the clumsy fishermen's trappings draped around the bunk. A fine web of scars over Barney's dark brows didn't mar his looks. His hands were lean and tanned as he pulled himself from the bunk.

3

"What is it, Pedro?"

"It is just that I would like to speak with you, amigo — alone. There is nothing to do for an hour. The crew is in the pens."

"What's the trouble?" Barney asked.

"I cannot talk to Cap'n Henry. But you — you are a guest aboard, you are not skipper or draggerman, but Barney Hammond. You were once fisherman yourself, Barney, before you became great prize-fighter — "

Barney laughed. "Okay, I know I'm just a guest package aboard." He felt a great affection for this old man who had played with him when he was just a child. "What's wrong, Pedro?"

Pedro spread his great, rough hands. "There is fog outside and danger in the fog."

Barney frowned. "Danger?"

"You came back to Easterly at a bad time, amigo. You know of the troubles on the waterfront? Cap'n Henry told you?"

"A little," Barney nodded. "Some strong-arm guy named Hurd is trying to rule the roost."

"Peter Hurd," the old man said. "An

4

evil man. He has brought hard times to us all. If a fisherman refuses to obey Hurd, something happens — poof! A man is knifed, a vessel's gear is wrecked, or she comes home with no fish in the pens and damages to be repaired. Next time the owner sails as Hurd orders."

Barney stamped into his cowhide boots. "What are you getting at?"

"It is trouble for your brother. Cap'n Henry fights this Peter Hurd and to avoid danger he fishes here, but he tells everyone he goes to Cashe's Ledge, thinking Hurd cannot interfere if he cannot find us."

Barney nodded. "I know about that. Henry told me that much before he went into his great silence." He grinned again. "Henry doesn't approve of me, Pedro. I don't think he's glad I came home."

"He is a difficult man to understand."

"And I'm not going to try any more," Barney said. "As for this Peter Hurd, he wouldn't try anything openly. There's a law against piracy after all."

"Hurd is the law in Easterly," Pedro muttered. "And there is fog on the sea. It is in my mind that Hurd knows where we

5

are, no matter what tales Cap'n Henry told ashore about our destination."

"How could he know?"

The old fisherman's big, brawny hand opened, revealing a key. "Someone aboard had this extra key to the radio. Someone used the radio to get in touch with Hurd."

"One of our draggermen?" Barney asked.

"A traitor," Pedro nodded. "A man who takes Peter Hurd's money. That is why I wait to see you alone, amigo. There is danger. We are helpless while we make this last set. And just now I heard something in the fog while I watched the winch — another vessel — "

"Come on," Barney said. "We'll see Henry about this."

"No, not I," Pedro said quickly. "You tell him. If there is someone in the crew who knows I told — "

Barney paused at the foot of the ladder, surprised. "Do you know who Hurd's man is?"

Pedro shook his head. "No."

Barney stared at the old man. *Superstition*, he thought. These old

Portugee fishermen were full of it. But if there was any truth in his fears —

"Where did you find this extra radio key?"

"An hour ago — under the mess table."

"Why didn't you speak up about it right away?"

Pedro looked disturbed. "I do not think too quickly. I do not know what it means until I hear that other vessel just now, out in the fog."

"All right. Thanks, Pedro."

Barney stepped out on deck and shivered in the bite of cold air. The fog moved around the schooner in long columns of vapor, leaving twisted alleys and lanes of clear air here and there over the sea. It was ten o'clock in the morning. A sea washed along the weather rail. He moved aft, passing Clee Duggan and the other DeFalgia brother, Carlos, at the main fish hold and glanced down the engine room hatch at Newfie Joe, the engineer, nursing his Diesel. The engineer's assistant, Carl Macklin, met Barney's eye and winked for no reason at all. Barney moved on to where the humming tow-lines hitched to the quarter bitts were swallowed in the turgid gray sea.

He paused at the pilot house door as the foghorn moaned. He didn't want to talk to Henry. He had tried hard enough to be amiable and helpful on his return to Easterly last week, even to the extent of coming along on this trip aboard the *Mary Hammond*. But apparently Henry never forgot or forgave and regretted sending him the letter. He shook his head, wondering if he would ever understand the man. They had nothing in common. He had hoped that their quarrel of five years ago, when he'd entered on a professional boxing career, would be forgotten by now. But not by Henry. To Henry the only things that mattered were the Hammond name and the sea. His desertion was not a matter easily glossed over.

Barney stared at the moving fog on the sea. The letter he had received from Henry in New York was the first since he had left Easterly. *It is not easy to say this*, Henry had written, *but I am in difficult straits, engaged in a struggle with certain*

8

waterfront elements here who are seeking to ruin me. I sometimes fear for my life. The criminals who run this town have broken me financially and if you could help in any way . . .

Barney smiled ruefully, recalling Henry's stilted Victorian phrases. He told himself he didn't belong here. Fishing was not for him. Maybe in the old days, with Gramps Barnabas and his Orient clipper ships, he might have made a go of it. But all that remained of the Hammond glory and wealth was this old schooner, shorn of her proud topmasts and converted into a Diesel-powered dragger and this had little attraction for him after New York and Lil and Gus Santini. He could almost hear the crowd noise around the ring and taste the heady exultation of his victories in the steady climb toward the middleweight crown. He'd get there yet, he told himself. It was too bad in a way that he'd lost his temper with Santini, his manager, and slugged him. But things would cool off eventually with the boxing commission and he'd be able to fight again in New York. It was bound to get straightened out. The only thing was, he'd made a mistake by answering Henry's letter with this self-imposed exile back in Easterly.

Barney opened the pilot house door and stepped in. "Henry?"

His brother glanced at him and turned away to continue his watch on the tow wires reaching out from the stern. "We'll be back in port by tonight," he said shortly.

"I didn't ask you that," Barney said.

"But that's what you want, isn't it?"

"Henry, I didn't come home to argue with you. Tell me about this guy Peter Hurd."

"That's no concern of yours."

"Why not? After all, you sent me that letter telling me about your troubles here. I simply want to help, if I can."

"You've made it plain that you're not interested in this sort of life," Henry snapped. "I regret sending you that letter. It was a mistake. We won't talk about it again. And now get out of my pilot house and stay out of my way."

Barney fought his trembling anger. He told himself to take it easy and he tried to look at his brother objectively,

10

without emotion. They didn't look much alike. Henry was tall and painfully thin with blonde hair and a narrow face and the hard, adamant jaw that Barney dimly remembered as his father's. Barney himself stood at five-ten, had his mother's dark black hair and eyes and a thick-muscled, chunky build that made him seem shorter than he actually was. Henry was eight years older. And the differences between the brothers went beyond their physical appearance. Henry was puritanical, fiercely in love with the sea and the heritage of the Hammond family; Barney was the rebel, the fun-lover, the wild one. To Henry, Barney's desertion to find a career in the prize ring was almost sacrilegious. He hadn't understood and never would.

But this was different, Barney thought. If Henry was in trouble on the waterfront, he wanted to help. You didn't just stand by and do nothing about a thing like this. He took out the key to the radio cabinet that Pedro DeFalgia had given him and dropped it on the shelf in front of Henry's tall, spare figure.

"This belongs to you," Barney said.

Henry looked at it and didn't touch it. "Where did you get this key?"

"Somebody used your radio to notify Peter Hurd that you're fishing close inshore like this."

"Who said that?"

"Pedro DeFalgia. He seems pretty worried about it."

Henry swung sharply away from the pilot window and stared at Barney. His face was distorted by cold rage, by a shocking intensity of emotion. His cheeks were drained white.

"What else did Pedro tell you?" Henry whispered.

"Nothing, Henry."

"You're lying!"

"Now, listen, skipper — "

"Damn you for listening to that crazy old Portugee!" Henry shouted. His lean figure trembled. "Get out of here!"

Barney was doubly shocked. The thought came to him that Henry was ill, crowded to the verge of breakdown by exhaustion. It still was not enough reason for Henry to talk about Pedro DeFalgia like this. The old men had practically raised them both in the big, empty house on Orient Street. He started forward, his own temper out of check and Henry suddenly swung at him, a wild, looping right that caught him by surprise, crashing into the side of his head. Barney staggered and fell against the schooner's wheel. His ears rang. Henry hit him again, his knuckles slamming the corner of his mouth. Barney tasted blood on his teeth and caught at Henry's arm.

"Henry, stop it!"

Henry tried to wrench his arm free. His eyes glittered. For an instant they wrestled dangerously in the narrow confines of the pilot house. Barney's strength was much the greater. Abruptly Henry stopped struggling and went limp. Barney held him for a moment longer until he was sure the spell of fury was over, then relaxed. Blood trickled from his mouth and down his chin. He wiped at it with a handkerchief, watching Henry with caution.

Henry leaned on the radio shelf. "I'm sorry, Barney."

Barney's anger was cold. "Forget it."

"No. I'm not myself. It's true I've been having a lot of trouble lately. I

13

haven't had a highline trip in months. The last three trips were failures and the crew is about to quit. I'm going to lose the schooner and the house, everything, unless things take a turn for the better. I'm sorry I lost my head."

"To hell with it," Barney said. He sucked at the blood that oozed from his lip. "I'll go back to New York as soon as we make Easterly."

"You don't have to do that."

"I'm not a fisherman and never will be. I've only made things worse by coming back here."

He pushed open the pilot house door and stepped out on deck. The foghorn brayed overhead, drowning his anger in waves of strident sound. The wet mist crept through the thin fabric of his coat and he shivered violently. He thought he heard an echo of the horn somewhere beyond the wall of white that surrounded the slowly trawling schooner, but he wasn't sure. For several moments he leaned on the salt-encrusted rail and struggled with his temper.

There was a shout from one of the men at the stern pens and he came toward the

14

pilot house and said something to Henry. The deck of the schooner trembled with the pulse of the Diesel engine. Barney listened to the man explain that the mark buoy had come loose from the drag. It was only a brightly painted keg used to mark the far end of the net when it was first paid out and he was surprised when Henry ordered Pedro and Carlos DeFalgia out in a dory to retrieve it. Pedro took off his red cap and scratched his thick, curly gray hair, then shrugged and went with his brother to launch the dory.

The pace of the schooner slackened until they barely maintained headway. The foghorn brayed again and Barney winced at the deafening sound. In a few moments the twins rowed the dory astern toward the drifting buoy, moving across a clear patch of water in the surrounding fog that twined over the oily gray sea.

It was only a few seconds afterward when he heard the throb of the other vessel's engines somewhere in the long, cotton-wool streams of mist. Here and there the wind had opened long alleys of clear water amidst the thicker areas

15

of fog and one such area was directly astern where the old men rowed in their dory. Henry and the draggerman on watch had no more warning than Barney. The horn screamed in sudden desperate alarm. There was a babble of voices from the crew around the pens and Barney paused at the fo'castle hatch.

He had half turned to go back to the pilot house when he felt the shock. Astern, a shape suddenly moved out of the wall of fog to port, plunging into the clear channel with reckless speed, the pound of the engine reverberating over the open water. Barney looked at the tiny dory out there, surrounded by the high walls of fog as if in the midst of a pond. He saw Pedro in his red stocking cap suddenly stand up in the dory and wave frantically. Then out of the opposite wall of mist rose a giant green bow that plunged for the *Mary Hammond*'s stern. Something bright and hard sheared across the towing wires. The deck trembled and the schooner's bow rose high on a swell as the towlines snapped. The gallows creeked and shattered. The foremast splintered with a scream of rending oak. Barney felt his legs knocked out from under him. He fell sprawling on the deck. The sea thundered over the rail and swept him headlong against the iron bulk of the winch. He grabbed frantically for support, closed his hands on a taut line and clung there in a welter of noise and pressure that threatened to drop him into the icy sea. Choking and gasping, he felt the *Mary Hammond* tilt crazily under him. Something struck across his ribs with stunning force. From within the depths of the stricken schooner came a high, wild, booming sound.

Barney struggled to his feet as the water subsided. His first glance was over the fantail. The fog was just swallowing the massive shape of the big green dragger that had swiped them. He looked for the DeFalgia brothers in the dory, but they were gone as if wiped off the surface of the sea by a monstrous hand.

One glance at the damage to the *Mary Hammond* sickened him. Disaster had come in a matter of seconds. The foremast was down, the gallows wrecked — and there was worse. The huge, costly linen net, cut free of the towlines, rose bubbling and frothing to the surface of the sea behind them. Fish glistened and thrashed in a mad circle, seeking escape from the torn netting. It would have been a rich harvest. But even as Barney watched, the mass of tangled line and fish sank in a seething foam beneath the next sea.

The *Mary Hammond* shuddered and righted herself.

Carl Macklin, Newfie Joe's assistant in the engine room, ran into him. The stocky man's face was ash-white.

"Did you see it?" Carl gasped. "Did you see what happened to the old men? The fog socked in right afterward, but I saw Pedro fall out of the dory. The dragger must've hit 'em."

"Are you sure?" Barney grabbed the panicky man's arm. "What about Carlos?"

Macklin's eyes were wild. "Gone! They're both gone!"

Barney ran toward the pilot house. The crew got out of his way, their faces stricken. Henry was slumped over the wheel, his eyes dulled with despair. He looked up at Barney's entrance and his voice was bitter.

18

"I should have known better than to take you along. You hate this vessel and the sea and you've brought bad luck to us. It's your fault those old men are dead."

"Now, wait a minute," Barney said. "You're talking nonsense."

"Am I? Maybe some of the fault is mine, too. I could have gotten along without you. You should have stayed in New York and not come back here to jinx the ship and my men."

"You asked me to come," Barney reminded him. "As for your superstitions — "

"I was in despair when I wrote that letter. It was a moment of weakness and I will not discuss it again." Henry's eyes glittered. "Now, get out of my sight. I've got salvage work to do."

"Aren't you going to look for the dory?"

"Aye. But we won't find it. Now, get out!"

Barney pushed open the door and walked to the rail. His head churned with memories of the two old Portugee fishermen. A sickness rose up inside him, blackening his mind. His thoughts

19

rushed backward to childhood scenes in a series of kaleidoscopic vignettes and at last he couldn't stand it and he walked aft, slowly at first, then faster and he was sick over the fantail of the crippled schooner.

2

BARNEY kept the shower water as hot as he could bear it, feeling as if he could never soak the cold touch of the sea out of his body. He was alone in the big Hammond house on Orient Street. He had left the schooner as soon as they made port, in darkness, jumping over the rail before the lumpers even had a chance to make fast the mooring lines. He had stalked off, speaking to no one, waiting for no one, anxious to escape the brooding atmosphere of tragedy that enveloped the crippled fishing boat.

The bathroom steamed with vapor as he stepped out of the old-fashioned tub with its ringed shower curtain and toweled himself vigorously. For six hours they had searched the fogbound ocean for a trace of the missing dory and the two old fishermen, but nothing had turned up. All the time, the foghorn had called in a forlorn voice, without hope. By nightfall there was nothing to do but jog so'sou'westward for Easterly Breakwater, the crippled vessel governed by her battered riding sail.

Barney frowned and dressed slowly then gathered up his clothes from the closet and began packing them into suitcases. His blistered hands were painful and he scowled at them. *Five years*, he thought. *I've been away from all this for five years.* His hands had carried him far from Easterly and the life of a fisherman. Magic hands, the sports writers called them. Barney Hammond, the Broadway Kid.

He finished packing, aware of the decaying emptiness of the big house all around him. Who did Henry think he was fooling? The house belonged to another century, another age, a time that would never come back. All these relics of Greatgramp Caleb, the whaling man, and of Gramps Barnabas, whose name Barney carried, and the two clipper ships Barnabas Hammond took to the Pacific for the China trade. It was all dead and done and over with. Henry lived with ghosts in a world that had ceased to be. If he was smart, he would sell the house and all the pirated junk in it and build himself a decent, modern dragger, since he was so intent on staying in the fish business. But even that wasn't what it used to be. The *Mary Hammond* was a Grand Banks schooner, built for cod. Now the schools of cod were way up to hell and gone along the Labrador coast, moving always northward as the water grew warmer up there and all that remained was the redfish — ocean perch, the freezing companies called it — and even the competition for that was tough enough to show the handwriting on the wall.

Barney moved restlessly through the empty house and turned into the library. It was after ten o'clock. Through the windows that overlooked the harbor, he saw the long finger of light from the beacon on Five Penny Island and the red blinker at the end of the massive stone breakwater. It was a good thing he got away from all this long ago. Otherwise, he'd have been tied up in the stinking fishery business just like Henry. It was all right for Henry. Henry liked it, believing in tradition. But it wasn't for Barney Hammond. The Broadway Kid. He looked down at his hands and clenched them. Those fists had battered his way out of the trap he saw himself in when Henry first ordered him out with the crew on a regular deckhand's shares. *What the hell*, Barney thought, *he wouldn't even give me a chance to go skipper*. And when Gus Santini, the fight manager, saw him working out at the Y, the way to escape had opened up for him.

Barney grinned wryly and turned away from the library window. Santini had turned out to be a crook, but that was all right. Even if Gus stole half the earnings, Barney still had a full kick. Not even Henry suspected how much Barney had socked away. Only Lil knew, because she always wanted to spend it. And he gave in to her, more often than not. Anyway, he had shown up Santini for the grafter he was. He laughed aloud, thinking of how he had planted one right across Santini's open, gaping mouth. He'd knocked the man's teeth into shattered splinters and dislocated his jaw. It was only a small portion of what Gus deserved, but he shouldn't have lost his temper in front of those witnesses. Now the commissioners were down on him and he was suspended indefinitely, because Gus had been too smart for him after all and he couldn't prove any of the things he'd told that crook.

Forget it.

Nobody here knew about it. They still thought he was going to fight Regan. He'd been given a real hero's welcome on his return, at Larry's Oyster House, which was the same old hangout, unchanged in the past five years. Easterly had paid a lot of attention to his ring career and this was his first trip home —

The telephone rang. He went to pick it up, thinking it might be Lil. She was supposed to have checked in at the Easterly House today, but he had called three times since leaving the *Mary Hammond* and she hadn't arrived yet.

"That you, Barney?" It was a man's voice, vaguely familiar. "This is Tal Carter, down at the Fish Pier. Wecome home, boy. Do you remember me?"

25

"Sure," Barney said. "You almost knocked the stuffing out of me once in the high school gym."

The man laughed, pleased. "I couldn't do it any more, Barney. Five years make a difference. It's great to have you back."

Barney had heard that Tal Carter was now the superintendent down at the Town Landing, where the fishing boats unloaded. He vaguely remembered him as a big, musclebound redhead who wore reading glasses.

"What's on your mind, Tal?" he asked.

"Well, I think there's going to be trouble down here unless somebody muzzles Henry."

"Why, what's he saying?"

"Listen, you know about Pete Hurd, don't you?" Tal didn't wait for an answer. "He came up here from Boston a couple of years back. Lots of money behind him. He practically runs the fishing fleet now, except for a few holdouts like Henry and some other old-timers. Henry thinks it was one of Hurd's boats that deliberately fouled his drag gear. He's saying that Hurd murdered the old DeFalgia men."

Tal Carter sounded anxious. "Barney, I asked Henry if I should call you and he said not to, but I figured you ought to get down here before trouble starts. Don't tell him I phoned, will you?"

"All right," Barney said. "I'll be right down."

The telephone clicked as if Tal Carter were in a hurry to ring off. Barney stood still for a moment in the big room. He looked at the table of Philippine mahogany where the telephone was kept. The table top was dusty. So were the bookshelves and the fireplace mantel. There was more dust on the glass encased ship models of Greatgramp's whaler, the *Bonny Lee*, and on Gramps Barnabas' clipper ships. Everything in this big house spoke of neglect and decay. Henry must have had a hard time to let his beloved possessions get run down like this, Barney thought. He didn't even have enough to get in a cleaning woman. He thought of the two old men lost in the sea today and suddenly he turned to get his topcoat. His resolution to help Henry just this once made him feel better. Then the telephone rang again.

The clerk at the Easterly House said: "Hi, Barney. Glad you're still up. The lady you were asking about just checked in."

"Good. Put her on."

"Sure thing."

Barney waited impatiently while he heard the desk clerk ask the switchboard girl to get Miss Ollander. He felt his stomach twist inside him. He hadn't seen Lil for almost a week and he missed her. Then he heard her voice.

"Baby?" he asked.

"Hello, lover," Lil said. Her voice was throaty and amused. "I was just about to take a shower. That train up from Boston belongs in a museum, doesn't it?"

"What made you so late?" Barney asked.

"I had some things to do. Come on over and maybe I'll let you scrub my back, lover."

Barney laughed. "In a little while."

"Oh? I thought you were so anxious."

"I've got to see my brother, baby. But wait up for me."

Lil said: "It will be difficult."

"What will be difficult?"

"Waiting, lover."

Barney laughed again. He felt better just hearing Lil's voice in this old mausoleum of a house. "How was everything in New York?"

"Everybody's talking," Lil said.

"About me?"

"About the way Gus Santini looks without his teeth. Lover, you have such a terrible temper. Would you do something nasty like that to me if you ever got angry with me?"

"Just don't give me any reason," Barney said grinning.

"But would you?"

"What has Gus been saying?" he asked.

"Come on up and I'll tell you," Lil said.

"As soon as I can."

He hung up, thinking of Lil Ollander and the way things were with them. He had heard lots of stories about Lil, but he preferred not to believe them. He knew her for himself and that was good enough for him. Having her come up here was the best thing he could have done. Maybe Henry wouldn't approve of Lil, but she'd

29

help him keep his perspective on this old home town of his.

A chill wind came off the dark harbor and up the hill to Orient Street. The Hammond house stood in the middle of the block between two old oak trees twisted by a century of sea winds. The leaves were already down, dry and crackling underfoot on the front lawn. Barney walked down the wooden porch steps and passed the smoothly worn iron deer that still decorated the front yard, then opened the grilled gate that led to the red brick sidewalk. The street was dark and deserted. In the summer, the night life of the town was enlivened by tourists, but by the end of September Easterly returned to its normal vocation of wresting a living from the sea. Looking down Orient Street, he could see the lights of the cannery and the quick-freeze plant on the State Pier far below. Both businesses were owned and operated by Malcolm Durand, who was said to control a half dozen other concerns scattered through the town, not excluding the Fisherman's Savings Bank.

Barney looked across the street at Durand's house and felt again the old tinge of animosity that had always existed between him and Mal. They had gone to school together, but whereas the Hammonds though socially among the most acceptable families in town were on the decline, the Durands had built up a fortune in the canning and quick-freeze processing of fish. They had both wanted the same girl, too, in high school days — Jo Lacey. After Barney left for New York, he learned that Jo had married Mal and moved into the big Durand house across the street.

It had bothered him for a long time. Then Lil came along and helped him forget it. There was no reason for him to think about it now. But he stopped on the dark, windy street and looked at the Durand house and knew that sooner or later he would see Jo again; he both welcomed the meeting and was afraid of it. There were lights on over there, but the draperies shielded the rooms within and he couldn't tell if anyone was there or not. He wondered if Jo knew he was home again. She hadn't telephoned.

Maybe she was avoiding him, because all she had to do was come across the street and ring the doorbell. Then he laughed, because he had forgotten that five years had gone by and they weren't kids any more and he couldn't expect Jo to chase after him the way she used to. If he wanted to see Jo now, he would have to pay a formal call. Maybe he would, he thought. And then he turned up the collar of his coat and walked quickly downhill toward the waterfront.

The Town Landing was opposite Five Penny Island within ten minutes of Orient Street although a whole stratum of society separated the closely packed old houses hereabout and the more dignified dwellings built by the ship captains of the last century. Barney crossed the familiar cobblestoned square into the glare of light that came off the wharf. A number of draggers were nested side by side at the near end of the pier, their dark hulls pitching restlessly in the chop of the harbor. To the left was a sail loft and a ships' chandlery and on the pier itself were the wharf building and sheds, brightly lighted, with a big painted sign that read simply *Peter Hurd, Fishery.* Barney frowned at the new name and walked faster, his heels rapping on the splintery planks of the wharf.

The *Mary Hammond* was tied up at the far end of the pier discharging the small catch she had made. The sound of the automatic conveyer belt, the clatter of ice and winches and the shouts of the lumpers blended with the redolent smell of salt sea and fish and brought the past back all the more sharply to Barney.

There didn't seem to be anything wrong.

The thought came to him for the first time that he was really home and this confused him, because his quarrel with Henry that caused him to leave town five years ago was due to his avowed hatred of the sea and the fishing industry into which he had been born. Barney shook his head and walked farther out on the pier.

Tal Carter saw him and came scrambling down the rickety outside steps from his second floor office. Tal had turned prematurely bald and had a little paunch that made his belt sag.

"Barney! Wait a minute, Barney!"

Barney paused. Tal came up to him and pulled at his coat sleeve until they stood in dark shadow beside the building, out of the glare of the wharf floodlights. Tal Carter's face was pale. "Did you see Henry?"

"I thought he was here," Barney frowned.

"He was. But he went up to Pete Hurd's office and I don't know what happened. You know Henry's temper, Barney. It's almost as bad as yours." Tal laughed weakly. "I guess you're not up on what's been happening around here."

"I'm learning," Barney said grimly. He looked up at the big sign that dominated the wharf. "Who is this Peter Hurd?"

"A newcomer with lots of capital behind him. And a squad of Boston goons who've been turning the waterfront upside down. It looks like a racket, but you know how Chief Petersen is — he can't even write out a traffic ticket, let alone handle a thing like this. There've been sluggings, accidents — even killings, some folks say, but they look like fishing

34

mishaps. Like the DeFalgia brothers. If you own a dragger, you either fish where and when Pete Hurd tells you to and sell at Pete Hurd's prices or something happens to you. Something bad."

"Hell," Barney said. "In Easterly?"

Tal nodded. "A few of the independent fishermen have been bucking Hurd's operation and the roof fell in on them. Cap'n Henry is one of the holdouts, of course. He'd never give in to pressure. Folks say Henry's got his back to the wall — some folks even thought he'd never get his schooner repaired after the last accident."

"He didn't mention any other accident," Barney frowned.

"Well, anyway, if Henry goes down, the waterfront belongs to Hurd. The thing that scared me tonight was the way Henry looked when he said he was going up to have it out with Hurd. He didn't even wait to get the lumpers organized unloading the catch. I told him to wait for you, but he wouldn't listen. He didn't even want to talk about you. I guess you couldn't make it up with him this trip, could you, Barney?"

"He's a fanatic," Barney said. "He thinks every Hammond must be a fisherman."

"Anyway, you'd better find him," Tal said.

"All right. Come with me."

"No, I've got to get back to the office. I'm sorry, Barney. It's my job. I can't take sides and get mixed up in this."

Barney looked at the man in surprise. Carter was afraid. It showed on his pale, round face, in the sudden sweat that glistened on his forehead.

"All right," Barney said again. "Thanks."

He waited until Tal ran upstairs to his superintendent's office again, then walked around the far side of the shed, away from the glaring floodlights where the lumpers worked. It was dark here. The clatter of the conveyor belts and the shouts of the working men were muffled by the long bulk of the intervening building. He walked along the stringpiece, his step light and sure on the uneven planking. To his right, the harbor water lifted and fell restlessly, gurgling and sucking around the old piles of the pier.

He was halfway to the other end of the

building when he saw the man crawling on hands and knees in the darkness against the shed wall.

Barney halted, unwilling to believe what he saw. This sort of thing didn't happen in Easterly. There had never been trouble like this before, not the way Tal Carter described it. He cursed under his breath and swung toward the crawling man and dropped to one knee beside him. It was his brother.

"Henry?" he said.

The man stopped crawling abruptly and in the darkness his face lifted, a distorted patch of white, to peer up at him. Barney sucked in a sharp breath as he got a good look at Henry's face. He started to put his arm around him to lift him to his feet and Henry struck out feebly in a defensive blow.

"Let me go!"

"It's me — Barney. Come on, Henry. Let me help you. What happened to you?"

"To hell with you. Stay away from me. You're no good."

Barney felt as if he had been slapped, but he didn't retreat. He forced Henry upright and leaned him against the wall, where the man sagged, breathing deeply, his head askew. Barney looked to right and left along the deserted edge of the wharf, but nobody was in sight. The wind moved darkly across the slip from the next pier, where a half dozen draggers creaked and tugged at their mooring lines.

The lower half of Henry's face was a mask of blood, his mouth was swollen and distorted and one eye was almost shut. Anger moved in Barney and made his voice harsh.

"Who did this to you?" he asked.

"What do you care?" his brother mumbled. "Take your hands off me."

Barney drew a deep breath. "I think you're trying to be deliberately difficult, Henry. Listen to me, once and for all. I didn't have to come back to Easterly. Maybe I had other reasons for leaving New York, but I could have gone anywhere else but this town and maybe I'd have liked it better if I had. But you wrote that you were in trouble and I came back. Ever since I showed up though, you've been trying to get rid of me again. I came here to help you, Henry, and I will. Now, who did this to you?"

"I'm finished," Henry muttered. "I'm wiped out now."

"No, you're not." Barney shook his thin brother angrily. "I'll stay here now, Henry. You understand?"

Henry stared at him, his ascetic face twisted in the gloom. He looked defenseless. "You'll stay for good?"

"I don't know. Until this is finished, anyway."

"You won't stay," Henry said. "You hate it here."

"I'll stay long enough to get this straightened out. You can count on it." Barney took a handkerchief and wiped some of the blood and dirt from the man's face. "Was it Peter Hurd?"

"Yes," Henry mumbled.

"Did you start it?"

"I guess I lost my head. I can't prove anything. You don't know how it's been around here lately, Barnabas." Henry's eyes glittered and he pushed aside the handkerchief. "It isn't just losing the DeFalgia brothers. I spent every cent

I had getting the *Mary Hammond* re-rigged and Hurd's dragger tore up every bit of it today. I haven't any more money to continue the fight. I can't outfit the schooner again. Besides, the rest of the crew is quitting. They're afraid of Hurd. So I'm finished and maybe you were right about the fishing business, after all."

"How much do you need for a new drag?" Barney asked.

Henry straightened, pushing away from the wall. He stared out at the winking red light on Five Penny Island.

"It will be more than the drag. Lots of other things. About six thousand dollars. I won't get it from the bank, because Mal Durand won't lend me any more. He wants to see me out of business, too. I might as well wish for the moon."

"I've got six thousand bucks," Barney said. "It's yours."

Henry stared at him. "You?"

"I haven't been fighting for peanuts," Barney said. "I've got quite a kick put away. You can have whatever you need, Henry."

"You're not fooling, Barnabas?"

"No," Barney said. He suppressed a smile. Henry was the only man who called him Barnabas. "Not any more, Henry."

"I'm glad," Henry said simply. He stood a little straighter. "I think I'll be all right now."

"Can you get home okay?"

"Yes. Let's go."

"I'm not going home yet," Barney said. "I'm going to see this Pete Hurd."

"No!" Henry said sharply. "He's got some strong-arm men up in the office with him. There were three of them altogether. You won't have any better chance than I."

"Listen," Barney said. "Are you sure it was one of Hurd's draggers that tore up your set?"

Henry shook his head. "I can't prove it. There was too much fog."

"Maybe a court of inquiry — "

"No. That's been tried. Carl Macklin took it to the Coast Guard, when his *Nancy M* was cut in two. Nothing was proved. The crew was intimidated and it was written off as an accident. But everybody knows it's Hurd trying to control the whole industry here by strong-arm methods. I never thought such a thing could happen here, but it has happened and it will continue until Hurd gets beaten or wins everything."

"I'll go up to see him," Barney decided. "You go on back home. I'll be back soon."

"Barnabas, I'm sorry I spoke to you the way I did. I'm sorry about a great many things I've said and thought. I — "

"Go on," Barney said. He felt sick at the changes he saw in Henry and his anger rose like a dark, bitter tide. He said again: "Go home, Henry. I'll only worry about you if you stay around here. I won't get into any trouble."

"Don't try to fight them, Barney."

"We'll see," Barney said.

3

HE got Tal Carter to drive Henry home and then turned back to the Town Landing and walked out along the pier once more. The lumpers were finished with the *Mary Hammond* and most of them had gone home. The floodlights had been turned out on the end of the wharf. Barney paused under the sign with Peter Hurd's name on it. It would do no good to go up there in a temper, he decided. He tried deliberately to control his anger, looking up at the lighted office windows. Hurd was still up there. Tal Carter had suggested calling the police, after one look at Henry's face. This was a personal matter, Barney argued, and when he refused he saw that Tal was actually relieved.

Barney went up the stairs on light, careful feet. Part of the building was used as a sail loft and the big, cavernous area yawned darkly to his right as he went up to the landing. Voices came from behind the closed door — a man's deep, booming laugh, a sycophantic chuckle and then a mutter of words he couldn't understand, muffled through the door.

He entered the office without knocking. A big man sat behind the desk, cleaning his fingernails with a fish knife. He had a square, dark face with a wide, thin mouth; his eyes were dark gray under thick, heavy brows. On the desk was a framed photograph of a new Boston dragger. On the wall behind him was an oil painting of a topmast schooner of the Thebaud class, rail down under a smother of white canvas.

"Come in," said the big man. "Don't bother to knock."

"I didn't," Barney said. He took his glance from the oil painting and looked at the two other men in the room. One of them was bearded, in fisherman's togs and cowhide boots. The other was as big as Hurd, in checked sport coat and square-toed shoes, with a broken nose and the scars over his brows that marked him as an ex-pug. Barney didn't know either of them. He turned back to the man at the desk. "You're Peter Hurd, aren't you?"

"I'm Hurd," said the big man. He took his feet from the desk top and waved to a chair. "Sit down. What's on your mind?"

"You," Barney said. "You bother me."

Hurd stared, folded his hands over the fish knife, and then laughed. "I guess I bother a lot of people, boy. They tell me I'm not too popular in this town. But I haven't seen you around, have I?"

"I'm Barney Hammond. You and your two goons here just beat hell out of my brother."

The big man sat a little straighter and glanced at his two men. Barney leaned back against the office door. Nobody moved. Then Hurd laughed again.

"Everything that happens around here, they blame me. You Easterly people are all alike. Just because you don't understand big business and want to stay back in the Victorian age, you think I'm some kind of monster or something. All I want is to do business here. Legitimate business." Hurd's voice suddenly hardened and he leaned forward

45

over the desk. "Your brother came in here and shot his mouth off like a crazy man. He couldn't prove anything, but I don't like to be told I'm a murderer. He got what was coming to him. I'm sick and tired of being blamed for everything that happens to these yokels when they go out fishing."

"It was one of your boats that deliberately ran across Henry's drag and tore it to pieces."

Hurd's eyes were flat and dangerous, but his voice was quiet. "Don't you know better, kid, than to come in here and say that?"

Barney said: "I'm saying it. You owe Henry a new drag."

Hurd grinned and shook his head. "You can take it to court, if you think you'll get any satisfaction out of it."

Barney said: "I'm not thinking of just the damages. I've seen plenty of operators like you. Cheap hoodlums who ride along on their muscle. I'm just telling you to lay off Cap'n Henry — or you'll face a murder rap."

Hurd got to his feet slowly, his eyes dark with anger. A loop of his thick gray

46

hair came down over his forehead. He kept his hands pressed down on the fish knife on the desk.

"I told you I don't like that word, kid. I don't like any part of it."

"I don't like it, either. But you bought it. You'll pay for it."

Hurd said: "I've got lots of men working for me in this town. But I think I know who you are now. You've been away, haven't you? The Broadway Kid, isn't that you? Pretty good middleweight — maybe even take the champ some day. You ought to stick to the ring, kid, and keep your nose out of something you don't understand."

"I understand mugs like you," Barney said.

Hurd's anger and puzzlement seemed genuine. "Listen, if your brother had a collision with an unidentified vessel at sea and a couple of his men got killed, that's nothing to me."

"Maybe I can make something out of it," said Barney.

For a long moment the room was filled with silent anger. Then Hurd nodded to his two men and gestured toward Barney.

47

"Throw this troublemaker out," he said. "He's as bad as his brother. They're both screwballs."

The two men advanced and grinned, their arms swinging. Barney ducked under the bearded man's reach and swung a hard right. The man grunted and fell back, arms outflung, fingers splayed wide. A trickle of blood wriggled down his bearded jaw. The second man grabbed at Barney. For an ex-pug, he was clumsy. Barney sank two quick lefts into his middle and drove him back. The man tripped over a chair and smashed it flat as he hit the floor.

Without warning, Hurd flipped his knife butt-first at Barney's head. He had no time to duck. The heavy bone handle crashed sickeningly across his eyes and he staggered to his knees. The bearded man came away from the wall and kicked him, his heavy boot slamming viciously into Barney's rib. Barney gasped and rolled desperately aside toward the door. He was filled with dismay at his carelessness. The bearded man kicked him again. Barney tried to grab at his boot, but his fingers slipped and he lost his grip. The pug came forward, laughing and knelt over Barney's body on his knees. Barney twisted his head aside as the man's heavy fist smashed down at his face. He heard Pete Hurd speak over the roaring in his ears.

"Let him up. He's had enough."

The pug straightened and Barney flexed his leg and drove his knee upward. The man screamed, a sound like the whinny of a horse, and rolled aside. Barney tried to scramble to his feet in the momentary respite. The bearded man caught him, hooked his left arm around his neck and ran him head-first into the wall. Barney choked back a sob of pain and frustration. The room spun around him and he sank slowly to his knees. *Now it comes*, he thought. *Now I get what Henry got*. Too late he knew that he had underestimated everything about the situation. Gus Santini, his manager, had always said he was too cocky. He was always warning him about bulling his way into things he hadn't weighed and judged. He wondered why he should think of Gus Santini at this moment. And he waited for the beating to follow his helplessness.

Nothing happened.

He looked up at Peter Hurd towering over him. The man had picked up his knife. He held it loosely in his left hand.

"I'm letting you off easy," Hurd said quietly. "Maybe you and your brother learned a lesson. Now shove off."

"Sure," Barney said. His ribs stabbed with pain when he straightened up. Blood trickled from a cut over one eye. "But I'll be back."

★ ★ ★

He had a drink at the Oyster House. Liquor didn't matter now. He wasn't in training for any future fights. His ring career was washed up and he needed the drink now more than he ever needed anything. It had been a long time since he broke training and the rum he chose seemed to explode in the pit of his stomach. It made him feel considerably better.

He knew he'd been a fool to plunge ahead and challenge Hurd the way he had. Especially after the example he'd seen of Henry. It was his temper again, he thought, and he wondered if he would ever learn to control it. Maybe Henry was right and it wasn't any of his business. He wasn't deluded by Henry's momentary softening to accept his offer to help. Henry was as unpredictable as the New England weather, a remote and stormy enigma of a man. Until today Henry had flatly refused to discuss his problems and had acted as if Barney's return in response to his letter of appeal was only embarrassing. Barney wasn't a fisherman and he hated the business, didn't he? Then why should he care what happened around here?

But he did care. From somewhere deep in his childhood came a stirring of loyalty, a knowledge that a man just didn't stand by and see his only family destroyed. What was done was done, he decided. He had offered to help Henry and he would.

John McCloy, the barman, said solicitously: "Another, Barney?"

"No, thanks. I've had enough."

"When is your next fight, Barney?"

Barney grinned painfully. "I just finished

one. The next isn't quite scheduled yet."

He paid for the drink and left, walking along the harbor front for two blocks and then cutting uphill toward the Easterly House. The hotel was Easterly's best, big and rambling, built on a rocky point that jutted into the north cove, with a view of the breakwater and the ocean beyond. In summer the little peninsula was a haven for artists and summer theatre people and the place hummed with activity. Now most of the cottages and wharves were empty, the studios closed and dark and deserted. Even Easterly House took on a touch of desolation in the dark, windy night. There was a restless crash of surf on the rocks below the entrance, and a bleakness to the dimmed lobby lights as Barney entered.

The nearness of Lil made his blood quicken and he paused to straighten his necktie in one of the mirrors in the lobby. One eye was slightly puffed and there was a cut on the corner of his mouth that would soon prove painful; but otherwise he decided he looked quite presentable.

The desk clerk grinned and said, "She's in 210, Barney," and would have held him up with talk about his fights if Barney hadn't been short with him. He went up the big stairway with quickened steps and knocked on the door to Lil's room.

"Come in, lover," she said.

"Hello, baby," he grinned.

She was beautiful. There was the polish of perfection to her grooming, a practiced art of posture and poise that made all her movements and gestures deliberate, just right. It took a lot of money to keep her like that, but Barney never thought about it. They were going to be married and she was in charge of the bank books and the savings account he'd had sense enough to start almost with his first professional fight. They'd done all right, he thought. He was proud of her, knowing that back on Braodway, at Dempsey's or Lindy's, heads always turned and tongues whispered when she went by on his arm. She was something to be proud of, all right.

She stood smiling quietly, knowing the effect she always had on him. She wore a pale blue flannel robe tied tightly about her waist and flaring in a full skirt around her hips and feet. Her long blonde hair had been combed loose and clung, shimmering, to her shoulders. Her voice was husky.

"Lover, it's only been a week," she said. "Don't look at me as if you'd never seen me before."

"You look wonderful," he said. "I can't help it."

"Then come kiss me."

He kissed her, thinking how swell it was of her to come up here to what must seem to her like the end of the world, just to join him in his involuntary exile from Broadway. Her mouth was warm and demanding. When he raised his head, she kept her hands on his shoulders and stared curiously into his face.

"What happened to you? Have you been fighting, Barney?"

He laughed. "Not professionally, baby. I got off easy."

"Then — "

"It was a thing for my brother," he said. "He's in a little trouble up here."

"I thought you and Henry didn't get along."

"We don't. But this is a family thing and I couldn't help myself."

"You didn't fight with *him*, did you?"

"No, no. Don't worry your head about it," Barney smiled. "Tell me what's new on Broadway."

Lil looked annoyed. She turned away from him and stared out through the window at the dark harbor. Barney glanced around the hotel room and saw that she hadn't finished unpacking. It was a big, comfortable room, one of the best that Easterly House had to offer. He wished he could stay here with her, but he knew that would be impossible in Easterly. He lit a cigarette and said: "Well, what's the matter, baby?"

"You and your temper," Lil said shortly. "Won't you ever learn to use your head instead of your fists?"

"This thing was something I couldn't help."

"I'm not talking about the brawl you got into here. I'm not that interested. But why did you have to go and hit Gus Santini the way you did? What did you think that would buy you, Barney?"

"Gus is a crook," Barney said flatly. "He had it coming to him."

"But he was crooked on your side,

wasn't he? What he did was for you — for us, to make more money."

Barney said flatly: "I won't fight for a crooked manager."

"But you couldn't prove anything about Gus, could you?"

"I told you about it before," Barney said patiently, "but I guess you didn't understand. It was about that fight with Tommy Forhan. Maybe I could have taken him and maybe I couldn't. That's the risk every fighter takes, unless he wants to keep punching at pushovers all his life and that gets a guy exactly nowhere. I needed that fight with Forhan and I needed to win, but I didn't want to win with the setup Gus arranged. Tommy's a good boy, a good boxer. I wanted to win fair and square, not with Tommy taking a dive because he had family expenses and Gus promised him a big cut to help pay hospital bills for his wife. I didn't want to win that way, Lil. Don't you understand? When Tommy let the cat out of the bag I got sore. That's all."

"And now you can't fight in New York any more," Lil said bluntly. "Does that help matters any?"

"I feel better about it," Barney said. "But let's not argue about this. It'll blow over, Lil. I'll get another manager soon and I'll be fighting all over the country. We'll see the sights all the way to Frisco and back, just you and me."

"Will we?" she asked blankly.

He stared at her. "Won't you come with me?"

"I like New York," she said. "All my friends are there." She turned abruptly. "Besides, how many fight managers are going to be willing to handle you after the way you treated Gus? It may take a long time to get a good connection, Barney. And what will we use for money until then?"

"Baby, you know we have plenty of money," Barney said. "As a matter of fact, I'm going to lend Henry six grand for his boat."

It was Lil's turn to stare at him. Barney thought she looked strange. For a moment something like panic flickered in her blue eyes. Then her mouth quirked and she began to laugh deep in her throat. Barney listened to her laughter and didn't understand it. He didn't see where he had said anything for her to laugh about. Looking at her, he felt a sudden stab of suspicion. But it couldn't be true.

"What's so funny?" he asked harshly.

Her laughter ended as quickly as it started. "You are," she said. "You're lending six grand that you don't have, lover."

"What are you talking about?"

"You don't have any money, darling. About eight hundred dollars, that's all."

Barney rubbed a hand over his face. He didn't believe it. It wasn't possible. "Lil, don't horse around with me," he said. "I figured we have over ten thousand dollars in the savings account. You told me so yourself only a couple of weeks ago. What happened to it?"

"It's gone," she said.

"How could that be?"

"Darling, don't look at me as if I stole from you?"

"Then where is it?" he demanded. "Where, Lil?"

"Sweetie, I'm expensive," she smiled.

"You mean you spent it?"

"I needed so many things, Barney. And I didn't want to bother you every time I bought something. After all, how was I to know you'd act so stupidly over Gus Santini and spoil everything?"

"Stupidly?" he repeated.

He felt incredulous and sat down abruptly on a corner of the bed. He wanted to slap her and the impulse shocked him. He trembled with anger as Lil came toward him.

"Darling, it's only money! Don't look so upset."

"I promised Henry six thousand dollars," Barney said dully.

"Well, maybe you can get it somehow."

She sat down on his lap and rumpled his thick dark hair. Her fingers scraped over the bruise on his eye and he winced. The softness of her body disturbed him as she knew it would. He had never been able to resist her. Lil had been something new and wonderful to him when he first hit New York. She was the lush promise of everything he had sought for in a woman — putting his tormented memories of Jo Lacey out of his mind, epitomizing the glamor and the reward he had dreamed of achieving in the prize ring.

She was working as a model and bit actress on TV when he first met her. Gus Santini introduced them. Gus said she was an old friend of his, the daughter of a man he had known long ago. There wasn't any reason to doubt it. Gus was twenty years her senior and his attitude toward her from everything Barney could see was purely paternal. Barney took one look at Lil Ollander and thought: *That's for me*.

Apparently Lil felt the same way about him. They went well together. She was good for him and even Gus had to admit that when Barney was in training, she had sense enough to leave him alone. She taught him about Broadway, what it meant and where it could lead, pointing out the people who were important and those who were grafters, thieves and hangers-on. She gave him the big-city poise and polish that he lacked and a plan for the future. It was Barney himself who suggested that she take care of their joint finances, knowing his own penchant for throwing away the money that seemed to flow so easily and copiously from Gus Santini's pockets. Everything was swell. Nowhere in the past five years had there been a hint of anything like this.

Abruptly he pushed her off his lap and stood up, stabbing out his cigarette in a tray. "Lil, what did you spend the money on?"

"Darling, there were so many things I needed — clothes and the rent on the apartment. All sorts of things."

"Ten thousand dollars' worth of *things*?" he rasped.

"Barney, I don't like your tone of voice."

"And I don't like what you've done to me."

She looked angry, then smiled and came toward him again and put her hands on his shoulders. "Lover," she pouted. "Don't be angry with me."

"Stay away from me," he warned.

"But, lover, I only — "

He slapped her. His anger broke over him in a wave and he had no control over it. It was as if his hand leaped out of its own volition, his open palm cracking sharply across her smiling face.

He had trusted her, building plans for a future in which she couldn't have had a real interest. Her only interest in him had been his money, in the things he bought for her. She had played him for a prize sucker. He slapped her again, blind in his rage and disappointment. She lost her footing and went down with a yelp of alarm and pain, crumpling to the floor. She held the side of her face with her hand and glared up at him.

"You stupid hoodlum!" she said.

"Get up."

"All your brains are in your fists!"

"That's right," he said. "And that's all you ever cared about — the money my fists earned for you. All that stuff about marriage and buying a house — that was all a come-on, wasn't it? All you did was con me while I let you keep the dough and trusted you. You must have had a lot of laughs while you spent it."

"Shut up," she said.

"I want that six grand, baby."

"It's gone."

"You can get it back."

"I can't!" she cried. "I spent it!"

"Who got it?" he grated. "Gus? Did

you and Gus split it?"

"No, it wasn't Gus."

"Somebody else?"

"No!"

He was suddenly sick with his disillusionment. He watched her get up warily and retreat toward the window. Her eyes scorned him. All these years, he thought, and he'd been acting like a blind fool. It took only a few days back here at home to regain his perspective on things. But he'd had it coming to him. He'd wanted to be the Broadway Kid and he had paid for it. His anger began to evaporate. If it hadn't been Lil, some other dame would have made a sucker out of him. He had been ripe for the picking.

"I'm sorry I hit you, Lil," he said.

"Are you?"

"It's just that I hate to let Henry down after I told him I could help."

She came toward him and kissed him. He let his hands hang at his sides, not touching her. He had no desire to kiss her or hold her. He wondered how he could have wanted her with that hungry desperation that had kept him blind about her for all these years. He didn't love her; he never had. But he didn't hate her now either. She meant simply nothing to him. "Barney," she whispered.

"Yes, Lil."

"You do love me, don't you?"

"I don't know."

"You can have the six thousand dollars for your brother," she whispered.

He looked at her. "How?"

"Promise you won't get angry again?"

"I won't get angry," he said.

"Sure?"

"Sure."

She turned away from him. "Well, the reason I took so long getting up here was that I knew you made a mistake, Barney, quarreling with Gus. Gus meant well. He was only trying to make sure of your successful career. So after you left town, I went to see him."

"Why? What's Gus Santini to you?" he asked.

"An old friend, that's all. And he treated me like one."

"Yeah?"

"He's not angry with you, Barney.

64

He knows how you feel and he's sorry the whole thing happened. He's not going to press charges or anything. He can't do anything now about the boxing commission, but you can fight anywhere else you please outside the state. He even went ahead and scheduled the Tony Reagan fight for you. For next week, if you're willing."

"No," Barney said. "I'm through with Gus."

Lil said: "But you want the six thousand, don't you?"

Barney didn't answer. He sat down and stared at the carpeted floor. It was quiet in the hotel room except for the muted crash and beat of the surf on the rocks below. He didn't know what to think. Too many things had happened in the past few days for him to get it all straight in his mind. Everything seemed to be coming at him at once. But he did want the money for Henry. The *Mary Hammond* was Henry's whole life. It was a matter of pride, too, that Henry must not think he had just been bragging and talking through his hat.

He looked up at Lil. The imprint of

his fingers glowed red on her cheek. He was aware of a sense of loss, an emptiness in him that echoed the shattering of the dreams he'd had about her. Nothing would ever be the same again, no matter what she said or how she behaved from now on. His love for her had been an illusion, like everything else, perhaps, in the past five years.

She was waiting for his answer.

"All right, Lil," he said quietly. "Where can I get in touch with Gus?"

Lil smiled.

"He's in the next room, lover. He came up to Easterly with me."

4

THE body floated at twenty fathoms, cold and rigid in the icy grip of the water. The old fisherman floated face down, arms and legs extended, still and blue, like a puppet turning gently in the fingers of the tide. The water was only a degree or two above freezing. It was black and cold. The eyes in the rigid blue face stared at nothing at all, seeing nothing of the ledge below, encrusted with little blue shellfish that welcomed the refreshing Labrador current and rejoiced in the return of winter. A glimmering school of reds darted toward the body and then veered off in sudden alarm as the current turned the stiff bulk over. The body bumped along the rocky outcropping and disturbed a patient sea skate. The current never let it rest.

The big, heavy-jawed cod was not afraid. His curiosity was aroused by this strange object that had intruded into his world. He moved his fins gently, gliding toward the dark bulk. He nosed at one heavy, twisted hand. The body rolled over again, floating toward the west. That was the way the current pushed it. The cod waited, seeing no life or danger in this stiff twisted thing.

Blood had come from a small bullet hole in the body. But death had been with this thing for many hours now and the cod was not interested. He backed off with an easy motion of his lateral fins and watched the current nudge the body off the ledge. For a moment it floated above the darkness of a deep, sandy pocket scoured out of the sea bottom. A bubble came from it. And another. The body floated slowly upward.

Far above on the surface of the sea, the great rusted buoy rocked and surged in the restless push of wind and tide. Its single cyclopean eye flashed monotonously in the dark night. It was the buoy marking Peter Shoal, thirty-two miles north-north-west of Easterly Breakwater Light. The buoy was a combination flasher and bell. Every now and then when an extra heavy sea pushed at it, the heavy bell gave voice *in a dolorous, brazen tongue, tolling over the dark waters of the water.*

Barney watched Gus Santini sign the check and wave it delicately in the air to dry the ink. Lil stood behind the fight manager, her hand resting on the man's shoulders. She smiled in a conspiratorial fashion at Barney. He didn't smile back.

"Three thousand now," Gus said. "And three after you fight Tony Reagan."

"The night of the fight," Barney said.

"Yes. Afterward."

"Before I go in the ring," Barney corrected.

Gus Santini laughed. "You drive a hard bargain, Barney. This Yankee air up here must have gotten back into your blood."

"Before the fight," Barney repeated flatly.

"All right. Before."

Barney took the check, glanced at it and put it away in his pocket. He stood up. Gus Santini smiled under his thin, hairline mustache and said: "You will be in shape for Reagan? He's a tough boy. He won't be an easy match."

"I'll be in shape for him."

"You want I should put some money down for you?"

Barney hesitated. "The other three grand. On me, to win. Give me the slips before the fight."

"Good," Santini nodded. "You'll double the money."

"I'll win," Barney said.

It felt hot and close in Gus Santini's hotel room. The windows were tightly shut, muffling the endless crash and boom of the surf on the rocks below. He felt impatient to get out of there. Gus's face still bore traces of his knuckles, showing puffy and yellow-purple around the mouth. But the man's air was friendly enough. They had shaken hands on the reconciliation and had a drink together. Lil had urged the drink on him, although he hadn't wanted it. He finished it now in two quick swallows and put the glass down. Lil came toward him and Gus Santini stood up smiling, his hand extended again.

"Are we friends, Barney?"

Barney looked at him for a moment. There was a time when Barney thought Gus was aces. He was a stocky man in his fifties with a youthful, sharp face and thick graying hair and a well-groomed look about him at all times. His eyes were dark and clever, his mouth mobile, smiling too much. Barney glanced at Lil. He felt nothing at all toward her. He shook Santini's hand briefly.

"All right, Gus."

Lil looked sulky when he left. She obviously had expected him to return to her room with her. But he didn't care now what she thought. He only wanted to get out of there.

A big Cadillac convertible was parked on the curving street in front of the hotel entrance. The street was dark and he couldn't see who was in it. But a voice called his name and he paused and then walked that way, breathing deeply of the cold, salt air. As he approached, the person behind the wheel leaned over and opened the door for him from the inside. He saw it was a woman. Then he saw that she was Jo Lacey Durand.

"Barney?"

"Jo," he said.

He knew he stood there grinning like an idiot, but he couldn't help himself.

She looked good to him. She looked wonderful. Five years had changed her from a slim girl in simple cotton dresses to a well-rounded, smartly turned-out woman. She wore her long, honey-colored hair in a coronet and a blue cloth coat was thrown over her shoulders. Under it, he could see a gray flannel suit with a gold pin on the lapel. She was smiling, too. Her hand was warm and firm in his when he slid into the car.

"Barney, I've been looking everywhere for you," she said.

"I had to come here on business." He saw that she was alone in the big car. "How is Mal?"

"Fine. He's looking for you down at the Fish Pier."

Barney frowned. "Now what's happened?"

"One of the DeFalgia Brothers is back in town."

"*What?*"

She nodded. "That's right. I know you thought they were both drowned this morning — it's been all over town — but it doesn't seem to have happened that way. One of them rowed all day and got ashore in the dory. He landed up the coast, just beyond Osterport, and a seine fisherman named Frank Colson pulled the old man out of the surf. It was Carlos DeFalgia."

Barney felt a quick measure of relief and thankfulness. "How did you find me here, Jo?"

"Just after Colson telephoned me — he was trying to reach Henry and the operator thought I might know where to find him — Father Dominic called and said that old Carlos had been at the church and was acting very strangely."

"How did he mean, strangely?"

"I don't know. But it worried me, so I asked the operator if she knew where to find you, because Henry wasn't at the house when I went over there." Jo laughed softly. "You must have forgotten what our Easterly telephone system is like. The switchboard girl knew exactly where you were. So I came over here for you and Mal went down to the Town Landing in case you happened to have gone there."

"Let's try DeFalgia's house on Portugee Hill," Barney said.

He sat back and watched Jo's smooth,

clean profile in the dim light as she turned the big Cadillac around in the narrow street. She wore a faint perfume that carried him back through the years to the time when she was always at his heels, dogging him with a young adoration that he had then found annoying. He wondered how many kinds of a fool a man could be in one short lifetime. Then he remembered the big car he was sitting in and it was as if cold water had suddenly been dashed over him.

"How is Mal?" he asked.

"Fine," she said. "Very prosperous. I'm the richest woman in town."

She didn't look at him when she spoke and her voice was flat.

"I didn't mean that," Barney said.

"I know you didn't. I'm sorry."

"You sound bitter, Jo."

"Do I? I'm sorry again."

"Are you?"

"Bitter? No. I don't like to think of myself as feeling that way, Barney."

"Jo," he said very gently, "I'm a friend. An old friend."

"I know. But you went away."

"I had to."

"I know that also. But I wish you hadn't."

"Perhaps it was a mistake."

Her smile was wry. "Let's not start off by talking this way. We'll get to it eventually, if you plan to stay here long enough."

They passed the Church of Our Good Lady of the Ship. The doors were open and the interior softly lighted, but in the brief glimpse Barney got as they drove by he didn't see Father Dominic. Up above in the bell tower, there was a lighted niche with a stone Virgin cradling a fishing boat in her compassionate arms. There was no sign of Carlos DeFalgia, and Jo drove by without slackening speed, turning the car up the narrow, cobbled street that angled sharply up Portugee Hill.

The house was a small, neat cottage set back from the street behind a picket fence, painted gray with white trim. It was a comfortable little house and it had served the two old men for forty years, even though no woman had ever had a hand in taking care of it. Carlos and Pedro had always kept it immaculate.

But it was no longer that way.

Someone had been here. Barney closed the brightly painted green batten door and dropped his hand from the wall switch. The light showed a complete disarrangement of the familiar old furniture such as he could never remember during his childhood visits. The disorder was an affront, an insult to the two old fishermen. It did not make sense. It looked like the work of a wild animal, burrowing and rooting about in a frenzy of abandoned destruction.

"Carlos?" he called softly.

Jo put her hand on his arm. He felt uneasy. It was cold in the house. He felt the tangible presence of something here that he did not understand. He walked through the room with its plush upholstered furniture and bright prints of old Portugal and entered the old-fashioned kitchen with its black iron stove and polished nickel trim. The back door was open. He closed it automatically.

Barney went all through the house with Jo following him and ended up in the bedroom. Nobody else was here. The disheveled house was terribly empty.

In the bedroom he saw that both sea

chests where the old men had kept their clothing and gear had been broken open, the beautiful brass locks smashed and vandalized. He listened to the sound of his own breathing in the room and shivered slightly. He went over to Pedro's sea chest and stared down at the rumpled clothing that had been pulled half out of it, spilling onto the floor.

Then he thought of something else and he opened the closet door and felt in the darkness of the topmost shelf, standing on tiptoe to reach in all the corners.

"It's gone," he said.

Jo was staring at him. "What's gone?"

"Pedro used to keep a tin box up here, with all his fishing and share accounts in it, and whatever papers he thought were important. Pedro was the clever one, Jo — you know that. He did the thinking for the two of them. Somebody must have come here and looked for the box and finally found it after turning the place upside down."

"But why? What could Pedro have had that was so important?"

"I don't know," Barney said. "It worries me."

It was more than just worry. He had a definite, tangible fear that something was wrong — wrong in an ugly, dangerous way.

Jo said: "How did you know about the box, Barney?"

"You know how I used to come up here to play when I was a kid, just to get away from the big mausoleum of a house of ours. I liked it much better up here and the old men used to spend a lot of time with me, telling me about the Azores and teaching me things that a fisherman should know. I saw Pedro working over his accounts lots of times. I know that tin box and I know where he kept it. I don't think he changed his habits in the time I was away."

"What bothers me," Jo said, "is why Carlos didn't come straight to the Town Landing to let everyone know he's safe."

"It bothers me, too," Barney admitted. "A lot."

He told her about Pedro's conversation with him early that morning on the *Mary Hammond*, about the radio key and the old man's fears that a traitor among the crew had informed Peter Hurd where they planned to fish. Jo's face was pale when he finished.

"Yes, it's been like that," she nodded. "Nothing is the way it used to be in Easterly."

"But doesn't anybody do anything about it?" he demanded.

"I can't," she said.

Something in her voice made him look at her sharply. Her chin lifted and her eyes met his. For a moment there was defiance in her clean-cut features, then she looked away again and her voice became listless and without hope.

"Everything here has changed since you went away," she said quietly. "Mal has changed, too. He isn't the man he was when you knew him. He likes the taste of power. He runs almost everything in this town except the waterfront — and he has plans for that, too."

"Wait a minute," Barney said. "Hurd has a lot of money behind him. Did Mal import him and his strong-arm men to win control of the waterfront for himself?"

The honey-haired girl didn't answer. Turning, she walked out of the bedroom into the kitchen. Barney followed her. A bottle of old Madeira stood on the scrubbed wooden china cabinet. Jo picked it up and handed it to him. It was empty. A glass, also empty, stood by the sink. Barney started to turn back to Jo, then saw the framed photograph of a handsome, dark-haired woman on the cupboard beside the empty wine bottle.

"Jo," he said. "Who is this?"

The girl glanced at the photograph in his hand. "Maria Rodriguez. She's a widow. Recently Pedro was paying a lot of attention to her. People said they expected Pedro to marry her."

"How long has that been going on?"

"A year or so. Why?"

Barney was troubled. "I don't know. How did Carlos take this romance?"

"He made it plain he didn't like it. He's been — he was very upset. It was really the only thing those poor old men quarreled about. Carlos didn't want to see the habits of sixty years broken up by what he considered an intruder."

Barney put the photograph aside. "You

didn't answer my other question, Jo."

"I know."

"*Is* your husband behind Peter Hurd?"

"Yes," she whispered.

"Who else knows of Mal's connection with Hurd?"

"Nobody."

"Are you sure?"

"Quite."

An alarm rang in the back of his mind. "And Mal is down at the waterfront now, looking for Carlos?"

"Yes, but — "

"And maybe Carlos is looking for Mal, too."

"I don't think — " Jo began. Then she interrupted herself and stared at him, her hand over her mouth. She whispered through her fingers. "Do you really think Carlos has connected Mal with Peter Hurd?"

"I'm sure of it," Barney said. "And if he feels that he lost his brother because of your husband's ambitions, then we'd better get down there and find him, quick!"

★ ★ ★

81

Jo parked the car on Water Street, a half block from the Town Landing. It was almost midnight. All the lights were out on the wharves except for the one on Peter Hurd's brazen sign. Jo's heels made a quick staccato sound as they walked quickly across the open cobblestone square. Nobody was in sight. The bars and stores in the area were closed and deserted. A little English MG was parked at the gate to the wharf and Jo said quickly: "That's Mal's car."

They turned aside and walked over to it, but the sports car was empty, the keys gone from the ignition. Barney straightened and drew a deep breath, aware of the tension tightening inside him. The wind blew in cold darkness from off the harbor. He felt Jo shiver as she stood beside him.

"Maybe you'd better stay here," he suggested.

"No," she said. "I'm going with you."

The *Mary Hammond* had been unloaded and lay in darkness at the end of the wharf. The pier looked entirely deserted except for the lights in Peter Hurd's office. Barney wished he had a flashlight. He told himself that he really didn't belong here, that none of this was his business. But he had made it his business and he couldn't step out of it now. Nor did he want to, when he thought of the troubles of the two old men and his brother. He owed them more than he could ever repay. He did not know what was in Carlos' mind, but he could guess. He knew how quick Carlos could be with that ivory-handled knife of his. The old man had not fought his way home against the strength of the sea for nothing. The thought made him walk faster.

The sail loft adjacent to Hurd's office was empty. He told Jo to stay at the foot of the stairs and went up quickly, taking the treads two at a time, his steps long and lithe. There was no sound from inside, but the lights shone through the pebbled glass panel in the door. He paused and looked back at Jo's dim figure at the bottom of the steps, then pushed the door open and went inside.

Nobody was there. He expelled his breath in a long sigh of relief and realized that he was trembling a little.

Jo watched him come down again.

"Is Mal up there?"

"No," he said. "No one."

"Did everything look all right?"

"Yes."

He pondered his next move. The presence of Durand's car at the pier gate indicated that the man himself couldn't be far off. But there was no sign or sound of him. Nor of Hurd and Carlos either. Yet he had the feeling that he was not alone on the pier. He wished Jo weren't with him. Her face was pale in the dim, winking light from the Five Penny beacon as they walked past the motionless conveyor buckets that slanted overhead from the ice house. In the dim starlight, the *Mary Hammond* looked like a dim ghost of her formerly graceful self. Her broken foremast had been removed and the tangle of debris from her ruined trawl had been piled aft by the fish pens, but the lovely curves and arcs of her spoon bow remained, a glimmering reflection in the restless black water. Barney felt a sudden twinge of pity for the fine old vessel and wondered at it.

Then Jo suddenly gripped his arm and halted.

"There," she whispered.

"What?"

"Somebody's there, by the forward hatch."

Barney studied the pattern of black and gray shadows on the vessel's deck. Nothing moved to disturb the geometrical rhythm of rigging and deck equipment. He moved forward, then jumped four feet down from the stringpiece to the schooner's planking.

"Catch me," Jo whispered.

She jumped lightly into his arms. For an instant she lingered in his grip, her body slim and firm, yet soft under his hands. Her perfumed hair brushed his face. Movement suddenly exploded from Barney's left and he let her go, spinning around toward the clatter of sound. A man's figure darted from behind the hatch cover and leaped for the wharf stringpiece above the schooner's rail. He ran with a curious limp to his left leg and his jump fell short by inches. Barney caught him as he fell back to the deck. He heard Jo's stifled scream as the man writhed free, arms flailing, his face a twist of terror in the starlight. He was no taller than Barney but stocky and solid, wearing a camel's hair topcoat that had a long gash ripped in one sleeve. Barney caught at his flailing arms and slapped the man's face hard, snapping his head back. The man fell against the heavy rail.

"Take it easy, Mal," Barney rasped.

"Let go of me!"

"Relax," Barney said. "Jo is with me."

The man stopped struggling. "Jo?"

He looked wildly about and saw the girl's figure on deck midway to the pilot house. Barney waited a moment, then eased his grip. Mal Durand didn't try to run away. He shuddered and sought to pull the torn flaps of his topcoat sleeve together with twitching, uncertain fingers. His mouth was slack, his breathing raw. His eyes were wild.

"What happened here?" Barney asked.

"Nothing."

"What are you doing aboard Henry's boat?"

"Looking for you."

"Did you see Carlos?"

"Who?"

"Carlos DeFalgia," Barney said patiently. "Is he here?"

"Yes." The man kept staring at his wife. "Yes, he's here."

"And Hurd?"

"No."

"Didn't you see Peter Hurd at all?"

"No."

"All right," Barney said. "Where is Carlos?"

"Below. In his bunk."

There was something wrong about the dark-haired man, something unnatural. He shook with terror. Barney examined him more closely. Durand had obviously been in some kind of a struggle, judging by the condition of his clothes. There was a smear of blood on the man's blunt jaw and more blood on his right hand. He saw that Jo did not come too near him and sensed an estrangement between these two even in this moment.

"What happened to you?" Barney asked.

"Nothing. I fell."

"You're lying," Barney said. "But let's go below."

87

Durand hesitated, then shrugged. He made a visible effort to pull himself together and he stopped shaking. Barney felt Jo's hand slide into his. Her fingers were cold. Durand led the way to the fo'castle hatch and went down the steep ladder with slow care.

Barney was not surprised by what he saw. An oil lamp was lighted, casting long yellow rays of uncertain light between the tiers of rough bunks. Carlos DeFalgia's bunk was in the starboard row, midway to the bulkhead that divided off the rope locker. Barney held Jo back, then swung ahead down the narrow aisle between the bunks. A red stocking cap that he recognized as Pedro's from early in the day lay on the rough, splintery deck. A man's legs in fisherman boots dangled over the edge of the bunk.

"Carlos?" Barney whispered.

He dropped to his knees beside the old man sprawled in the bunk. Carlos had his older brother's square, swarthy features and thick, curly gray hair. The dim oil lamp had drained the usually healthy color from the fisherman's face and made it look shrunken and waxy.

At first glance, he thought the old man was dead.

The bone handle of a knife glimmered where it stuck out of the draggerman's side. The heavy peajacket was caked with salt and blood. Barney could not suppress a shudder. He felt a sudden, desperate anguish for the man in the bunk.

"Carlos?" he whispered again.

The old man opened his eyes. He recognized Barney. His lips moved and he whispered for a moment in Portuguese, then said: "My brother Pedro is dead, senhor."

"I'll get a doctor for you, old friend," Barney said.

"No, senhor. Listen to me. Pedro is shot. With a gun."

"What are you talking about?" Barney asked.

"Is not me. Is my brother. Shot."

Barney was confused. "How do you mean, shot?"

"Pedro is not lost in the sea by accident. He is murdered, Senhor Barney."

"But — "

The old man's lips moved, whispering again in Portuguese that Barney could not understand. The sound had a ghostly sibilance in the dim light of the bunkroom. Barney heard Durand's footsteps behind him and straightened, looking at Durand finger his thin dark mustache.

"What's he saying?"

"Carlos says that his brother Pedro was shot at sea, from Hurd's boat, I think, while they were in the dory. I don't understand it. Do you know who knifed him?"

Durand looked at the old man. He didn't seem to hear Barney's question. The man in the bunk had seen Durand and for an instant his eyes glittered with a deep and infinite hatred as they fixed on Durand's white face. He raised one hand and then closed his thick fingers around the ivory handle of the knife stuck in his side. Before Barney could stop him, the old man made a convulsive effort and pulled the knife out of his body. He held the bloody blade as if he were going to throw it, then it suddenly slipped from his red fingers and clattered to the deck.

The old man was dead.

5

BARNEY hit the bag viciously, *one-two, one-two-three, one-two*. He enjoyed the impact that thudded up through his shoulders. He enjoyed the sweat that glistened on his half-naked body. He worked out with a savage intensity, as if by physical effort he could dull the bitterness of his thinking and forget his memories of two old men who had died for what seemed to be no reason at all.

The Y had been practically empty when he first got down there this morning, but a small crowd gathered to watch him within a half hour. He had been in training in New York up until last week and he knew himself well enough to realize that he had been honed to a razor sharpness and that all he had to do until the fight with Reagan down in Boston was to keep himself there. But that was easier said than done, he thought. He wasn't interested in the coming fight. He couldn't keep his mind on it.

He kept hitting the bag, taking out his frustration on the padded canvas. No matter how hard he worked at it, he kept thinking of what had happened last night.

Chief of Police Petersen had been worse than a flop. All that interested him was to wield that big brush full of whitewash, slapping it over everyone concerned. He wasn't concerned with the murder or with getting at the truth of what had happened. All that concerned the big, moon-faced cop was to establish what did *not* happen, namely, to insist that Malcolm Durand and Peter Hurd had nothing to do with the death of the old man aboard the *Mary Hammond*. It was easy to see in whose pocket the police department fitted. Durand had everything in the bag — his money bag, that is.

Barney had argued about it with a rising temper. He had almost gotten himself thrown out of the police station after being threatened with a cell for himself, until Mal Durand interfered and checked the chief's anger, too. Durand was smooth and easy and confident in the way he managed things — a man who knew the power of his position and exercised authority with a quiet assurance that left no doubt about what he wanted done. And yet he managed to keep from being too obvious about it.

One-two, one-two-three. Barney gave the bag one last left, then turned and walked away from it. Jo Durand was standing in the doorway to the gym. He ignored the little knot of spectators and threw a towel across his shoulders as he went toward her.

"Good morning, Barney," she said.

There were faint violet smudges under her fine eyes. She looked as though she hadn't slept much. The sunlight tangled with her warm, honey-colored hair.

"Hi," he said.

"I heard you were down here," she smiled. "I wanted to come and thank you for not — for respecting my confidence last night."

Nobody was within earshot. "About Durand and Hurd?"

"Yes, Barney."

"I didn't mention it because I can't

see how it can be proved," Barney said. "Anyway, it's obvious Mal has the cops in his pocket and anything I said would probably be held against me. But if and when I get some proof, I'll have to come out with it, Jo."

She nodded. "I know. But there isn't anything you can do, Barney."

"I'm not so sure of that."

She regarded him with somber gray eyes. "Please, don't interfere in this. You'll only get hurt."

"Are those your words or Mal's?"

"Mine," she said without hesitation. "Please."

"I'm sorry. I can't promise anything."

She looked hurt, but he knew that she understood. Then she smiled briefly. "Come to dinner tonight — you and Henry. Mal wants to talk to you."

"I'll bet."

"Will you come?"

The thought of seeing Jo preside as wife and hostess at Mal Durand's table bothered him. It bothered him a lot. He didn't know why it should. A long time ago he had adjusted himself to the knowledge that she was Mal Durand's wife. It shouldn't disturb him now, but it did.

Gus Santini came in the gym door with Lil on his arm. Barney noticed the change in Jo's face. It became more formal and her chin stiffened. News travels fast in a small town, Barney thought grimly. Jo gave him her gloved hand.

"Please come," she said.

"I'll see."

He watched her leave the gym, a trim, straight figure in a neat gray suit, with her long legs moving proudly. Lil turned her head to stare after her. In contrast to Jo, Lil looked a little too well preened and sophisticated at this hour of the morning. Barney wondered why he should even compare the two girls, considering how he and Lil had been with each other until last night. He felt a momentary confusion and then Gus adjusted the towel over his shoulder and walked toward the shower with him.

"Glad to see you up and working this morning," Gus said. "I hear you had a session with the cops until all hours."

"Yes," Barney said.

"How did the workout go?"

"Fine."

"You want to train here for the next week until you fight Reagan?"

"That's right."

"Lil thinks we should move somewhere to the Berkshires. There's a nice camp I could get for us. We could get there today. Maybe this home-town trouble isn't too good for your peace of mind, Barney."

"I'm all right," Barney said bluntly. "I'm staying here."

Lil frowned. "Because of her?"

"Jo and I are old friends," Barney said. "We went to school together."

"And played post office, too, I'll bet."

"Maybe."

"I think we ought to go to the Berkshires," Lil said. "You have too many distractions in this town. And I hear you're in trouble with the local cops."

"Not yet," Barney said.

"Do you plan to be?" Lil asked coolly.

Gus intervened, his voice anxious, his hands on their arms in a placating gesture. "Break it up, kids. Barney's got enough

96

on his mind just thinking about Reagan. Lil, you ought to know better. Barney, get your shower and get dressed. I got a little surprise waiting for you outside. A little convertible I picked up. You can use it while you're here."

"Fine," Barney said. He appreciated the gesture and suddenly felt better. "I'm sorry, Lil."

"So am I, lover."

He kissed her briefly and went to the shower room, where he stood under the hot water for a long time, not thinking about anything at all, his mind deliberately blank. He took half an hour to dress, listening to Gus and Lil talking outside the locker room. They were waiting for him, but he didn't want to spend the rest of the day in their company. He had other things to do. A back door to the locker room led to the fire-escape exit and solved his problem. He knew Lil would be angry, but he could explain it afterward.

A green convertible Ford was parked around the corner from the Y, the keys in the ignition. It was the car Gus had gotten for him. He got into it quickly, hoping he wouldn't be spotted by Lil or Santini, and drove away fast.

It was a fine, clear September day, much warmer than yesterday. The sea sparkled a deep, rich blue. The sun felt good on his face as he turned toward the highway that led up the Easterly River. On the far side of the river were long, grass-grown dunes, with here and there a closed summer cottage. About four miles up he came to the shipyard where the *Mary Hammond* had been towed this morning. The sound of caulking hammers thudded in the clear air. There were two draggers on the ways being refitted for the winter fishing season off Norfolk, Virginia, and on the third marine railway was the *Mary Hammond*, a crew of shipwrights busy removing her broken foremast. He recognized Henry's tall, spare figure high up on her deck, watching every move of the workmen with an anxious eye. Barney climbed one of the ladders leaning against the schooner's hull.

Henry looked as though he'd had no sleep at all last night. His face was gaunt and haggard in the noonday sunlight.

Barney hailed him across the racket of the hammers and the steady chugging of a donkey engine nearby and Henry turned quickly to greet him.

"Have you got the money?" he asked immediately.

Barney grinned. "Part of it, skipper. Three thousand bucks." He took Gus Santini's check out of his wallet and gave it to Henry. His brother's hands shook as he took the check. "That ought to take care of getting the work done, anyway. The rest of it and maybe more will come when I fight Tony Reagan next week."

Henry looked grateful. "I think I may have misjudged you, Barnabas. You can't know how much this means to me."

"I have a small idea," Barney said. "But forget it."

"I will not," Henry said. "I guess I've behaved pretty badly about your coming home. But if you hadn't — well, I'd be through."

"Never mind," Barney smiled. "You're welcome to the money and anything else I can do." He looked across the broad, littered deck of the schooner. "I guess I'm fonder of this old girl than I thought."

"Are you?" Henry asked quickly. "Do you mean that?"

"Sure," he said, a little embarrassed by Henry's intensity. "Why shouldn't I be?"

"I'm grateful."

"And you're also exhausted," Barney said. "You ought to be in the sack today. You didn't get any sleep last night, did you?"

"I'm afraid not."

"Where were you when Carlos was killed last night?"

Henry looked startled. "What do you mean by that?"

"Well you weren't at home when the cops tried to get you. You didn't show up at the police station until an hour afterward."

"I know. I was walking around, trying to think of what I could do to get the *Mary Hammond* repaired. I guess I didn't really believe what you told me, about getting the money for her."

"What about the DeFalgia brothers?" Barney asked. "What do you think it's all about, Henry?"

"I don't know. I wish I had the answer myself."

Barney said: "I can't get it out of my mind. Chief Petersen isn't going to do anything about it, that's plain. But I feel as if I owe those two old men something for everything they did for me as a kid."

"You keep out of it," Henry said sharply. "It doesn't concern you, Barnabas. It's none of your business."

"I'm going to make it my business," Barney said.

Henry started to reply again, then abruptly brought his thin lips together in an uncompromising line. Barney didn't press the subject. He felt satisfied to leave things the way they were with Henry. He hadn't been on such an amicable footing with his brother since he'd left Easterly and he didn't want to spoil it now by appearing stubborn. Henry liked to feel that he was still the older brother, the one to give the orders in the family. It was a question of habit and it wasn't easy to break. He knew that Henry was struggling hard to be pleasant and he was content to leave things at that.

He watched the progress of the workingmen on the schooner for several more minutes before he left. Half an hour later he was in Chief Petersen's office in the Town Hall.

Ira Petersen was a fat man who wheezed as he sat down in his green padded swivel chair behind his desk. He was neither intelligent nor competent, but he was a great political handshaker and he suited the Easterly electorate well enough. He had been a fisherman for most of his early years, a prerequisite to any political office in town and he ran routine matters fairly well. But he was obviously out of his depth in a case of murder.

He regarded Barney with small, wary eyes.

"You sort of got under my skin last night, Hammond, with some of the things you said about me. It wasn't very kind. After all, you've been away from this town a long time and you didn't have no call to throw a tantrum about the way I'm conductin' this investigation. I hope you feel a little more calm about things this mornin'."

"I do," Barney said. "I'd just like to know what progress you've made so far."

Chief Petersen wheezed. "You can read about it in the Easterly *Times*, son."

"Have you gotten anywhere?"

"We're lookin' into some leads we got. A thing like this, boy, you can't rush around yellin' your head off and expect the killer to be frightened by the sound of your voice into comin' in with a signed confession. Way things look, this might take a little time."

"How much time?" Barney asked.

"That's hard tellin'."

"Until Mal Durand gives you the word?"

Petersen's fat face turned red. He shuffled some papers on his desk with thick, pudgy hands. It was warm in the office. The chief of police looked uncomfortable with his broad bottom securely fitted to the upholstered swivel chair.

"There's no call for you to talk like that, Hammond. I told you so last night."

"But Durand pulls the strings around

103

here, doesn't he?" Barney insisted.

"I admit no such thing. Mal is a fine businessman, one of our leading citizens, but he has no more influence with our justice than the next man."

"You can tell that to the voters," Barney jeered, "but not to me. He calls the tune and you dance to it. And the tune he's calling for now is for you to quietly give this whole case the deep six."

Anger made the cop's jowls tremble. "You got no call interfering, boy. It's none of your business."

"That's what everybody has been telling me. But I liked those two old men. They were fine, harmless, hard-working citizens in this town and somebody killed them both."

"We ain't so sure about that."

"I told you what Carlos said to me. Pedro stood up in that dory yesterday morning and tried to signal that dragger off and he was shot. Carlos tried to grab him and all he got was his red woolen cap. The body sank out of sight."

"Exactly. So we got no proof that what Carlos told you is true."

"That's right," Barney said. "But you've got Carlos' body in the morgue and you've got the knife that was stuck into him."

"His own knife," Petersen said.

"You're not implying he killed himself with it, are you?"

"The police don't jump at conclusions, boy. We need more evidence." Petersen put his fat palms down on the desk. His eyes and his voice were mean. "We know those two old men had quite a row before they went out on that last fishin' trip. They lived together for almost sixty years and all of a sudden Pedro decides he'd like to get married. That kind of upset his brother. He seen all his nice comforts go out the window with a woman in the house. They had a pretty hot argument about it."

"So what?" Barney asked.

"So maybe they was still arguin' in that dory," Petersen said quietly.

Barney stared at the man, disgust rising in him. "Are you suggesting that Carlos killed his own brother and threw him out of the dory?"

"It's an idea," Petersen said.

"And maybe Pedro swam ashore, or maybe it was his ghost, and stuck a knife in Carlos to get even with him?"

"Maybe," Petersen said blandly.

Barney fought with his temper. The thought came to him that perhaps the chief was stringing him along, because nobody could be expected to swallow the stupidity that had just been voiced. But he wasn't sure. He might be underestimating this fat-cat of a cop. It was obvious that Petersen was not alarmed by his questions. The man was very sure of himself, confident of the power behind him. Barney felt as if he were butting his head not against a stone wall but against the fat, springy suet of the chief's big belly.

The chief stood up, his breathing asthmatic. Through the window behind him Barney glimpsed the soaring flight of a gull.

"The best thing you could do, Hammond," said Petersen, "is stick to your own knittin' and leave police business to the properly constituted authorities. You got no business buttin' in and interferin' like this. I'm goin' to overlook the accusations you made to me last night and today, but I feel I got to give you a warnin' to make you realize this is serious. I won't tolerate any more of your talk. You keep it up and you'll regret it."

"How?" Barney asked. "Will you tell Durand I'm a bad boy?"

"I can take care of my own washin', boy."

For an instant the chief's face lost its slack, fatty look and became hard and dangerous. Barney had the sudden feeling that perhaps Petersen's big belly was not as soft as it seemed. The man was dangerous. It didn't bother him or frighten him. He met the chief's stare with a grim look.

"Are you warning me off?" Barney asked.

"I'm tellin' you to keep your nose clean and stay out of this thing."

"And if I don't?"

"Then it's your funeral," Chief Petersen said.

6

BARNEY drove the long way around to Easterly House, since he had no relish for Lil's temper when she discovered how he had left the gym by the back door while she waited for him. He had no desire to see her and intended to maintain only such contact with Gus Santini as was necessary until the fight with Tony Reagan. He didn't even think of Reagan or the problems involved in that direction. He drove up Portugee Hill, stopped for lunch at a little restaurant that catered to fishermen and learned from the counterman where Maria Rodriguez, the widow, lived.

The house was set back a little from the street and a neat red brick walk led up to the porch and the front door. The place was only two blocks away from the DeFalgia cottage. An old maple tree spread twisted, naked limbs over the red shingled roof and from the back yard Barney could see the blue harbor with its heavy breakwater and the white lighthouse shining in the sun. It was a peaceful New England coastal scene, repeated a score of times in the little fishing towns strung up and down the coast. Yet there was something special about Easterly that made it mean more to Barney than anywhere else. The thought surprised him and he walked up the porch steps and rang the bell with annoyance.

He listened to the bell pealing somewhere deep inside the house. A squirrel scrambled along the limbs of the maple tree and chattered in scolding tones. There was no answer to the bell and he rang again, then stepped back and looked up at the second story bedroom window. He was in time to see a flicker of movement behind the lace curtains of the north window.

He waited.

Nobody came to the door.

The squirrel stopped chattering and ran back out of sight somewhere behind the house. Leaves rustled on the lawn, crackling dryly. A dragger nosed around the breakwater and headed toward the fish pier, its white wake a long trail growing dim out in the wide horizon of the sea. Barney shivered for no reason at all.

Turning, he strode away from the house, down the neat brick walk to the street, then walked around the block and up a wide sandy lane to the back of the widow's place. He couldn't think of any good reason why the widow should pretend she wasn't at home. Church bells intoned over the town. It was one o'clock. There was a small back porch leading to the kitchen door and Barney crossed the lawn with quick steps and went soundlessly up the wooden stairs to try the door. It wasn't locked. He let himself quietly into the kitchen and closed the door behind him.

The woman saw him and gave a little scream and almost dropped the liquor bottle. She had already poured a tumbler half full of rye.

"It's all right," he said quickly. "I'm Barney Hammond."

She made a nice recovery, sliding the bottle out of sight on the china cupboard and moving the glass behind some others that stood on the shining porcelain sink. When she looked at him, her eyes were still frightened, but she had command of her voice.

"I don't care who you are," she said. "Get out."

She had a nice voice. Barney was pleasantly surprised, because she was so much more attractive than he had expected. It was the woman whose photograph Jo had shown him in the DeFalgia house. But she didn't look like a widow and she was somewhere in her middle thirties.

"You're Mrs. Rodriguez?" he asked.

"Get out," she said again.

"Maria Rodriguez?"

"I'll call the police," she said.

"I've just come from there," he told her.

"Are you a policeman?"

"Chief Petersen and I understand each other," he said. "There's nothing to be afraid of. I just wanted to talk to you. Why didn't you answer the bell when I rang before?"

She didn't reply. She looked at the

tumbler of liquor on the sink and then glanced quickly away. Her eyes were frightened. She was a handsome, black-haired woman with a full breasted, smoothly rounded figure in a trim red dress tightly belted about her narrow waist. Her eyes were dark, bright and alert under long arched brows. In profile, her face was delicate yet firm, classic in the small nose, full mouth with rounded chin, only a slight sag under the chin betrayed her maturity. A number of surprising thoughts flickered through Barney's mind as he studied her. This woman didn't look like the prim, middle-aged widow who might be attracted to an old bachelor like Pedro DeFalgia. He wasn't surprised now that Carlos had objected to the romance. This dame was out for whatever she could get and more. Barney's thoughts shifted to adjust to this new perspective. There was something hard and predatory about Maria Rodriguez that would have made a sucker out of poor old Pedro if he'd ever lived to marry her. Maybe he was lucky not to have reached his goal, at that. This was the sort of woman who devoured men, he thought.

Her voice was harsh and challenging.

"Well, have you seen enough?"

"I'm sorry," he said. "I didn't mean to stare. I was just surprised, Mrs. Rodriguez. I somehow got the impression that you were much older."

"I don't think I like that," she said.

"I'm not sure I like it either," he shrugged.

"I know what everybody has been saying about me and Pedro," she went on. "And it isn't true. I tell you, it's a lot of rotten lies! Pedro and I had an understanding. We were going to be married. He was a fine, sweet old man and he'd have taken good care of me. Is that such a bad thing for a woman like me to want?"

"It all depends."

"To hell with you," she said.

Barney walked across the kitchen and picked up the tumbler of liquor and handed it to her. "You might as well drink this. You'll feel better."

She shrank away from him as he approached. "Don't you come near me."

"I don't bite."

"I want you out of my house," she said.

"After we talk a bit," Barney replied matter-of-factly.

"I don't have anything to say to you! You have no right — "

"What are you afraid of?" he asked again. "What has scared you like this, Maria?"

There was no question about her fear. She shook her head mutely, her eyes regarding him with an animal wariness, as if she were ready to run if he moved an inch nearer to her. He didn't try to get closer to her. He put the liquor glass down on the kitchen table. It was quiet in the house. Everything seemed peaceful and normal. He could hear the quick, uncertain sound of her breathing.

"Listen, Maria," he said. "I've been told that none of this is my business, but I think it is. I liked Pedro and Carlos DeFalgia. I want to know why they were killed and who did it."

"I don't know anything about it," she said quickly.

"I've been away," Barney told her. "I'm not acquainted with the latest developments in this town. But those two old men meant a lot to me and I don't like the manner in which everybody is trying to bury them and forget them. I shouldn't think you'd feel too happy about it either."

"I'm not," she whispered. "But there's nothing I can do."

"You could answer my questions," Barney suggested.

"But I don't know anything!"

Barney said: "Tell me about Pedro. You must have seen him a lot and you must have noticed anything odd or strange about his behavior. Usually if a man does something or has something in his possession that's dangerous, he knows it and worries about it. Did Pedro seem upset or strange to you?"

"I — no."

"But he was worried about something, wasn't he?"

"I don't know."

"Wasn't he upset about my brother's feud with Peter Hurd?"

"He never talked about it."

Barney shifted ground. "When were you going to be married?"

"In about a month." Her voice was surer. "I know most people think I was marrying him just because he's supposed to have saved up a lot of money — he and his brother, I mean — but it was really more than that. I was really fond of him." Then she looked hopeless again. "But I don't expect you to believe me."

"Maybe I do," Barney said. "More than you think. You visited his house, didn't you, Maria?"

"Occasionally."

"Did Carlos resent you?"

She smiled for the first time. "A little. But I could handle Carlos. We would have gotten along all right."

Barney wondered about it, looking at the woman's ripe figure. He said: "You know about Pedro's tin cash box, don't you?"

"I — I heard it was stolen."

"You knew where Pedro kept that box, didn't you?"

"No!" she said sharply.

"Who told you about it then?"

"I — one of the policemen. They were here this morning. I think it was Chief Petersen."

116

"Did anybody tell you to keep quiet about what you knew?"

Her reply came too quickly. "No! Nobody!"

"I think you're lying," Barney said. "I think somebody's thrown a good scare into you. Was it the chief?"

"No."

"Peter Hurd?"

"No!"

"Or Mal Durand?"

She shook her head mutely. Her face was white and terror-stricken and her fingers worked at her throat. Overhead, a floor board suddenly snapped and creaked. The woman's head jerked up and she stared at the ceiling, her mouth open. Then she looked quickly away. There was someone else in the house. Barney was suddenly sure of it. He stood very quietly, listening, but the sound was not repeated. He felt the hair prickle on the nape of his neck.

Barney looked at the frightened woman and spoke very quietly: "Who is it?"

"It is nothing."

"Somebody's up there."

"No. Please. It is no one." Her voice

gathered strength. "Please go. You will only make trouble for me. Please be kind and go away."

"After I look upstairs."

"I'll tell you anything you wish to know — "

Barney paused halfway across the kitchen. "Why were the DeFalgia brothers killed?"

Her face was tormented. "Honestly. I don't know."

"Then why was Pedro killed at sea as Carlos said he was? Why did they pick such a time and place?"

"I can't tell you. Believe me! I wish I knew."

"Did you see Carlos when he came back to town last night?"

"No."

"Did you know he was back?"

"Not until this morning, when the police came."

Barney felt frustrated. He was sure the woman was telling the truth in some respects, but he was equally certain that she was keeping something back, forced into silence by her obvious terror. He looked up at the ceiling once more, but all was silence up on the second floor of the house.

"I want to see who you're hiding upstairs," he said.

"You mustn't. It is nobody!"

"I'll see for myself."

He wasn't prepared for the woman's violence. Her fear had disarmed him. He was almost to the kitchen door when he heard the sudden sharp crack of broken glass. He spun around and saw that she had broken the whiskey bottle on the edge of the sink. She held it by the neck and the jagged edges sparkled with sharp, splintery lights. Her face was transformed, desperate, enraged.

"Put that down," he said hoarsely.

"Get out!"

He hesitated a moment, then made as if to go on through the door. The woman jumped for him. Twisting, he caught at her wrist and the impact of her body drove him against the door jamb with a thud that shook the frame house. Her body was lithe, tigerish. Her eyes looked crazed. For an instant the force of her leap drove the broken bottle toward his face. He twisted desperately, felt the glass graze his cheek and then his leverage on her wrist forced the ugly weapon aside. Another ounce of pressure and she dropped the broken bottle with a sharp moan of pain.

"Now behave," he gasped.

The woman was limp under his grip. He watched her for a moment and saw that her resistance had gone out of her as quickly as it had come. Turning, he walked through the house and started quietly up the stairs.

7

ARNEY was halfway up when the man appeared at the head of the steps.

It was Malcolm Durand. He came out of the shadows of the upper hallway, his body thick and oddly aggressive against the dim background, his face momentarily blurred, an oval of white that stared down at Barney's tall figure. His hands hung empty at his sides. He wore a dark blue suit, and his thick hair was neatly groomed. He touched a finger to his neat little mustache and said: "It will not be necessary to come up, Hammond."

"All right," Barney said. "Come down then."

He backed away to let the man descend the staircase. Maria Rodriguez had not come out of the kitchen. He thought he heard a quick, stifled sob from the back of the house, but he didn't take his eyes off Durand.

The man moved into the small, trim

living room as if he were quite familiar with the house. Barney followed, his mind racing to try to add up this new connection between the town's richest man and an unimportant widow. But maybe Maria was not as unimportant as she seemed. In any case, there was something to be learned here.

Durand was quietly in command of himself.

"It is regrettable that you discovered me here, Hammond," he said. "But really not so difficult to explain."

"I'm listening," Barney said.

"I really don't have to explain anything, but I don't want you to jump to any wrong conclusions."

"Of course not."

"I'm as interested in discovering the reason for this murder and the identity of the murderer as you are."

"Why not leave it to your fat boy, Petersen?"

Durand's handsome face was bland. "I am personally interested in this matter just as you are," he said.

"What did you hope to learn from Maria here?"

"I wasn't sure. Anything that might throw light on this question."

"And did she tell you anything enlightening?"

Durand stiffened. "I don't like your tone of voice."

"I'll change it when you tell me something concrete."

"As I said. I owe you nothing."

"What about Maria? Are you the one who threw a scare into her to keep her mouth shut about what she knows?"

"No. Certainly not!"

"But somebody intimidated her," Barney said.

"Yes, that is obvious. But she told me no more than she told you."

There was a thin red welt on the man's forehead from the wound he had suffered the night before. Barney stared pointedly at it.

"Chief Petersen was aware of your sensitivity yesterday," Barney said. "He didn't ask you to explain what you were doing on the *Mary Hammond*."

"I told you. I was looking for Carlos DeFalgia before that crazy old man caused trouble."

"So now Carlos was crazy?"

"He wasn't normal, I should think, considering the wild tale he told you about his brother being shot in the dory. If anyone wanted to kill Pedro, why not do it ashore?" Durand smiled. "It would have been much simpler and easier that way."

Barney frowned. "Then you don't believe that Carlos told me what he did?"

"I'm sure you repeated exactly what Carlos said. But I think Carlos was mistaken. He was filled with the idea of vengeance, his mind fixed on the thought that the accident at sea yesterday was deliberate and therefore the direct cause of his brother's death. I don't see why we have to complicate matters with any fancy or wild tales about Pedro being murdered. Pedro's death was a pure accident. But Carlos didn't think so. And Carlos came to the Town Landing in search of revenge."

"Looking for Peter Hurd," Barney said flatly.

"Perhaps."

"Or you."

"Why should he have looked for me?"

"Because Hurd is your man," Barney said.

Durand was startled. "Who told you that?"

"I think it's obvious. The money behind Hurd and your aim to run everything in this town — you and Hurd go together like two and two."

"That's ridiculous."

"I intend to prove it," Barney said.

Durand's dark eyes glittered. He touched his mustache again with the little finger of his left hand, the gesture delicate and deliberate. When he spoke, his voice was equally light and deliberate.

"You are just as stubborn, bullheaded and stupid as you always were, Barney."

"You don't deny that I'm right though?" Barney grinned.

"Of course I deny it. And I think a little word of advice is in order."

"If you're going to tell me to mind my own knitting, then you'd better save your breath," Barney said. "Everybody seems anxious for me to sit on my hands and do nothing about what's going on in this town and the more I hear of it, the more convinced I am that if I don't do anything about it, nobody will."

"But perhaps, for Henry's sake — "

"What about Henry?" Barney demanded.

"He's just as involved as anybody else. And if you have any desire to spare your brother — "

"Henry loved those two old men as much as I did."

"Of course," Durand nodded. "But Henry was in deep trouble. His struggle with Hurd was getting worse every day. His fishing trips were failures and he was completely out of money. He came to the bank for a loan and I had to deny it on the grounds that he was a bad security. He completely lost his temper and acted like an insane man. There were plenty of witnesses. He was vile and abusive and it was only because of Jo's feelings that I pressed no charges. But I had to have him removed from the bank by physical force."

"Maybe Henry had the right idea," Barney said. "But that still doesn't involve him in these murders."

"I wouldn't be so sure," Durand said quietly. "I am simply trying to point out that if your persist in rooting around for trouble, you may find some in your own back yard."

Barney hesitated. The warning was plain enough. And Mal Durand seemed very sure of himself. He tried another tack.

"That cut on your forehead that you got last night," he said. "Who gave it to you?"

"I told you I fell."

"Maybe your stooge, Petersen, accepted that, but I don't. If you had fallen anywhere on the deck of that schooner, your clothing would have showed it. The schooner had been at sea for six days and it was pretty dirty, covered with fish scales and rime that would have stuck to your coat. But you weren't dirtied that way at all. So you didn't fall down and cut your pretty forehead. Was it Carlos with his knife who did that?"

"No."

"Someone else?"

"All right!" Durand drew a deep breath and seemed to come to a sudden decision. "It was the murderer," he said quietly.

"You saw him?" Barney asked.

Durand shrugged. "Not much of him."

"But what you did see of him?"

"He had already ambushed Carlos and stabbed him. I heard something going on aboard the schooner while I was on the wharf and went aboard. I was taken by surprise and attacked. It was dark and I saw very little."

"Who was he?" Barney demanded.

"I couldn't say."

"You can't — or you won't?"

"I didn't see enough of him to be sure."

"But enough to give you ideas about his identity?"

"Perhaps." Durand smiled, very sure of himself now. "It will do you no good to question me like this, Hammond. Unlike you, I'm not given to going off half-cocked about things I know nothing about. I will do nobody an injury by making wild guesses. What I suspect I will keep quiet about until it can be proved. I think I have been patient enough with you now."

The man's sanctimonious air was repellant, but there was nothing more Barney could do. He stepped back, frustrated, as Mal Durand walked past him and out through the front doorway. He waited for a moment, oddly disturbed by what Durand had said and then turned back to the kitchen.

Maria Rodriguez sat in one of the chairs near the window. Her hands rested quietly in her lap. She glanced up at Barney's tall figure, then went back to staring at nothing at all.

He didn't speak to her. He went out the back way and paused in the little yard that overlooked Easterly Harbor. The dragger he had seen rounding the breakwater just before he went inside was now making its way through the inner harbor to a private anchorage several wharves down from the Town Landing. Barney watched it for some seconds without actually seeing it. Then his eyes suddenly widened and he swung around the house and walked rapidly toward his car.

8

TWELVE miles southeast of Osterport Light, the body floated in thirty fathoms, rigid and frozen under the dappled sunlight that touched the surface of the water. The tide and current had worked at it steadily for twenty-four hours, moving it this way and that but always closer to shore, as if the body itself were driven by some remorseless, inflexible purpose.

The bullet wound in the back was almost indistinguishable now. The woolen mitten on the right hand had come off and the heavy, rope-hardened palm was turned up in a gesture of supplication. There was no answer from the sunlight that sparkled on the surface waves above. There was nothing but salt, cold and silence and the slow wavering of the sea bottom's vegetation.

Twenty feet from where the body floated, atilt on the sandy shelf below, was the bony, twisted skeleton of the

Orpheus. The *Orpheus* was a small brig of about eighty tons built for the coastwise logging trade down from Maine. She had been launched in 1843 and had gone down with all hands in a storm in 1860. She had rested undisturbed for almost a century now, content with the quiet darkness and the murmuring tides that scoured the sea bottom.

The body drifted toward the ancient wreck. It turned and twisted, as if seeking to avoid this obstacle that suddenly loomed in its path. The current which had been an almost sentient and reasonable factor in helping the body along its course now turned traitor and implacably drove the corpse against the vessel's hull. There were several bumps and a number of fish, startled from their nests in the labyrinth interior, darted out and fled streaming away through the layers of bright and dark water.

The body rose, floated over the moldering taffrail and struck the broken butt of the mainmast, then caught on a rusted finger of iron that protruded from the splintered deck. It tugged as if in irritation, seeking to free itself.

A woolen scarf had come loose from around the dead man's neck and floated like a snake above his head, then drifted down and wound itself around the iron bar. The body was made fast, securely anchored to the dead hull of the old vessel. It turned slowly, twisting like a trapped creature at the end of a line. It could not get free. The face turned upward toward the shining surface of the sea. The face was blue and frozen, the lips skinned back from the old, yellowed teeth in a grimace of rage and pain. The eyes glared upward with baleful fury.

* * *

Tal Carter looked up at Barney and speared a clearance sheet on a file spike and shuffled papers from one side of his cluttered desk to the other. He looked embarrassed. His bald head shone in the bright afternoon sunlight that came through the dusty panes of his wharf office window. A rhythmic clattering noise came from the Durand Cannery across the ship and the steady chugging of a donkey engine somewhere was clear

132

in the September air. Carter's round face perspired. It was hot and stuffy in the office, opposed to the limpid blue of the sky and sea beyond his windows.

"Barney, listen," he said. "I wouldn't advise you to go there."

"I suppose you're going to tell me it's none of my business, too," Barney said.

"Well, is it?"

"I'm making it my business. You know how I felt about those two old men. And from what I've learned already, this thing is bigger than anybody suspects."

"Look, I've been thinking," Carter said. "If what Carlos said is true and Pedro was shot at sea from the dragger, then you're faced with more than one killer. Somebody else killed Carlos when he came ashore."

"I haven't figured that out yet," Barney admitted, "but it's possible. There's too much I don't know to make any guesses now."

"On the other hand," Tal went on, making his voice reasonable, "it's possible that Carlos was out of his head and didn't know what he was saying."

Barney frowned. His jaw was stubborn.

"I still want to look at the dragger that just came in. And I want to know who owns it."

Tal Carter sighed. "Peter Hurd."

"He's the owner?"

"That's right. He bought the *Lucky Q.* from Sol Alvarez."

"Where was he fishing?" Barney asked.

Tal Carter pawed his pile of papers with ink-stained hands. The fingers trembled a little. "Here it is. *Lucky Q.* Middle Bank."

"Thanks," Barney said. He started out of the office, then turned back. "One other thing you can help me with, Tal. Who is this Maria Rodriguez?"

Carter grinned. "Quite an armful of woman, I'd say."

"Is that her reputation or just your wishful thinking?"

Carter grinned again. "Me, I guess. I never heard anything about her. But you know how this town is. She came here from Provincetown — at least, that's what she told the grocer and other shopkeepers she dealt with. A widow. She keeps pretty much to herself."

"But she stepped out enough to hook

134

Pedro DeFalgia."

"Yeah, I guess she did."

"Know how they happened to meet?"

"Hell, I wouldn't know that, Barney." The wharf superintendent looked serious again. "Look, Barney, if you're going over to the *Lucky Q.* be careful, huh? Hurd's crews are usually a tough bunch."

"I'll be careful," Barney promised.

The dragger he sought was moored at a pier only ten minutes' walking distance from the Town Landing. A new board fence, freshly painted a bright red, had been erected across the street entrance to the pier. The gate in the middle of the fence was padlocked and a sign read, *No Admittance*. The fence was too tall for him to see over, but he could hear the noise of unloading from beyond its blank height. Barney banged on the gate, got no answer and walked on down to the next pier, an abandoned relic that stuck like a broken finger into the harbor water. There was no barrier here. He walked out on it carefully, picking and choosing his steps among the broken, gaping planks. His course paralleled the other pier with about sixty feet of sluggish water between them. His view was clear and unobstructed. He noted the repairs and paint that had been applied to the pier sheds and the big sign that dominated the seaward approach, a duplicate of the one at the Town Landing that brayed forth Peter Hurd's name. Then his attention shifted to the dragger that had been moored to the other pier.

* * *

It was a big, powerful, Diesel driven craft with Boston lines, painted a glaring green. The name, *Lucky Q.* was in gilt letters on the high, sharp bow. That bow looked familiar, Barney thought. It could be the boat that had torn up the *Mary Hammond*'s drag gear in the fog. He watched the men working around the fish holds, getting ready to unload the catch. Nobody seemed to have noticed him. He squinted at the dragger across the glare of water, studying the sharp, high bow in particular, but the sunlight that reflected off the ebbing tide made his vision deceptive. He had to get closer to it — aboard it, if he could.

The low tide had uncovered a narrow strip of junk scattered beach and two skiffs were drawn up on the coarse sand. Barney walked to the pier entrance and jumped lightly down to the littered beach. One of the skiffs had a hole in the bottom and was obviously rotting apart, abandoned there. The other looked serviceable enough and a sculling oar rested in the thwarts. Barney shoved it into the water and stood up, balancing himself toward the stern and tried to recall the sculling skill he'd had as a boy.

There was still no alarm as he moved the skiff out into the water between the two piers, angling toward the bow of the green dragger. He was halfway there when his suspicion became an excited certainty. The bow of the *Lucky Q.* was brass-sheathed, painted over with the same bright green as the rest of the hull. But just above the water line the paint had been deeply scored and here and there a glint of the original brass shone through. Barney worked the sculling oar a little faster. The hull of the dragger loomed over him as he closed in between the bow and the private pier. Abruptly the skiff drifted into an area of strange, forbidding shadows. He put out a hand to fend off the impact of his little boat and grabbed at the massive bow of the dragger.

His hand came away wet with green paint.

He almost laughed in triumph as he stared at his smeared fingers. Then a voice hailed him from overhead and he glanced sharply upward.

"Shove off, mister!"

Peter Hurd's blunt, hard face peered down at him from over the rail of the *Lucky Q*. Barney grinned and held up his green-stained hand so that the man could see it clearly.

"I'm coming aboard," he called.

"And I say you shove off!"

Barney hesitated. There was a ladder leading up to the stringpiece of Peter Hurd's private wharf, but it was about twenty feet back toward the shore of the pier. He didn't relish trying to climb it in the face of the big man's boots.

"When was the paint job done?" he called up.

"Yesterday," Hurd said blandly.

"After this boat rammed the *Mary Hammond*?"

"We tangled bows with the *Dolphin*. You'll find her tied up at the State Pier."

Barney balanced himself against the rise and fall of the skiff under his feet. "Is the *Dolphin* another of your boats?"

"She is," Hurd nodded. "Now shove off, mister!"

Barney looked at the fresh paint on the dragger's bow again. Frustration brought the edge of anger over his mind. He looked up once more at Hurd's grinning, hard features. He knew at once what had happened. The conviction that this was the dragger that had rammed Henry's schooner was unshaken, but Hurd had moved quickly and smartly to forestall any embarrassing questions of investigation. He had rigged an accident with another of his boats to cover up the scars made on the *Lucky Q*. By keeping the difficulty within his own fleet, he forestalled any outside investigation by the marine insurance companies. But the whole thing only served to make

139

Barney more certain that he was on the right track.

Other faces appeared alongside the dragger's bow rail with Hurd. There were too many of them, Barney saw, and he decided that discretion was the better part of valor. Besides, he had already learned what he wanted to know. Considering the way Hurd moved to cover up the evidence, he wasn't sure what he could do with his new knowledge. But every little bit helped.

"You shove off peaceably, mister?" Hurd asked. "Or do we accidentally drop an anchor through your thick skull?"

"I'm going," Barney said. "Thanks."

"For what?"

Barney grinned and didn't answer. Hurd looked troubled for a moment as Barney sculled his little craft backward and then turned toward the shore again. His back tingled when he turned the skiff around and manipulated the oar through the stern oarlock. He didn't like to turn his back to a man like Peter Hurd, ever. But nothing happened.

Ten minutes later he was parked in the car Gus Santini had lent him, about fifty feet from the locked pier entrance. Water Street was narrow and twisting, following the shoreline. On one side were the piers and wharves, on the other were ships' chandleries, bars and tumbledown, gray, and weathered structures whose business defied analysis. There was a bar almost directly across the locked gate that he watched. It seemed to do quite a good business. Barney settled himself down to a long and patient wait.

After an hour the gate opened and two men came out, walking toward the Town Landing. They went by the car without noticing Barney. One of the men was Peter Hurd. The other was the booted and bearded fisherman who had helped beat him up the night before. Barney's knuckles tingled as he watched the two men walk away up the street, but he remained in the car, watching for the rest of the crew.

It was growing dark when the *Lucky Q.* completed unloading. The gate was thrown wide and half a dozen men clumped out to the cobblestoned street. Two of them turned north away from the parked car, heading for their homes.

The other four went into the bar as if drawn there by invisible strings. Barney remained where he was, comfortable in his patience.

A neon sign went on over the bar entrance. A juke box began to pulse from inside the building. One of the four men came out after only ten minutes. Barney waited. The street was totally dark now except for a lamp at the far corner and a protective floodlight over the pier gate. The floodlight was fine for Barney's observation. It showed up the faces of the other two fishermen who came out of the bar at six o'clock. That left only one in there, a determined man about his liquor. Barney got out of the convertible and went into the bar.

The bartender nodded, put aside his newspaper, then went back to it as Barney waved him down. At first he didn't see anyone else in the bar. The juke box stood against the back wall, a glowing, throbbing monster that beat out a polka with insatiable rhythm. There were wooden booths back there, stained a dark mahogany and the lights were negligible in little orange shades. Barney walked to the rear and found the man he wanted in the last booth. The bartender followed him.

"He's got troubles," the barman said. "He does this every trip since he sold the boat. When he finishes the bottle, I'll take care of him. He lives upstairs."

Barney looked at the man in the booth. The bottle was half empty in front of him. He was a small man with a dark, weatherbeaten face etched by sorrow.

"Has he got a name?"

"Sol Alvarez. Used to own the *Lucky Q.* that just came in. You want to drink something, mister?"

"Ale," Barney said.

"One ale," the bartender said and he went away.

Barney slid into the booth across from the fisherman. He felt good about this, considering it a break. He couldn't have chosen a better man to question. Alvarez lifted his blank gaze from the shining bottle and stared back at Barney. His thin face twisted. His narrow shoulders were hunched in his peacoat. Dark, liquid eyes sorrowfully considered Barney's big chest and sports jacket and bow tie.

"You wish to drink with me, sir?"

Barney said gently: "Do you remember me, Sol? I'm Barney Hammond."

"Who?"

"Barnabas."

"The prizefighter?"

"That's right," Barney said. "Only I'm home now."

"Go away," said Alvarez. "Go away quick."

The barman brought Barney's ale. It was dark and nutty in flavor. He sipped it slowly, watching the fear in the fisherman's dark, sad eyes.

"Why should I go away, Sol?"

"I am not supposed to talk to you."

"Who told you that?"

Alvarez poured his tumbler half full from the whiskey bottle. "No one."

"Was it Peter Hurd?"

"He is my employer now."

"He stole your boat from you, didn't he?" Barney asked.

"No. Yes." The fisherman sighed. "I no longer know."

"The *Lucky Q.* is his now, isn't it?"

"I am not alone in my misfortune. Other men have lost their boats, too. It is bad luck, perhaps."

"Not just luck," Barney said. "You know that."

"Nothing can be done about it now."

"You can talk to me," Barney said.

"No."

"Are you afraid?"

The dark eyes lifted to his face and fell again. "Yes. I am very much afraid."

"Of Hurd?"

"Yes."

"He told you and the rest of the crew not to say anything?"

"There is nothing to say, Barney. Go away."

"Not until you answer my questions."

"You will only cause trouble for me."

The fisherman lifted his glass to take a long drink. Barney reached across the table in the booth and took the glass from the man's shaking fingers. For a moment Alvarez resisted him. Then his fingers went slack and Barney put the glass aside.

"It's easy to fight the bottle," Barney said. "It's more of a job to fight a bastard like Peter Hurd."

"I cannot fight. I am beaten."

"You can tell me what happened on the *Lucky Q.* this trip."

"Nothing happened!"

"You rammed my brother's schooner," Barney insisted.

"No!"

"And somebody shot old Pedro DeFalgia from your boat."

"No! Give me my drink."

Barney said softly: "Answer me first."

"You are crazy. Nothing happened."

"That's a lie," Barney said. "Answer me."

"We had an accident with the *Dolphin.* That is all."

"After you tore up the *Mary Hammond*'s nets?"

"No. Nothing like that happened."

Barney said: "Weren't you a good friend of Pedro's?"

"Yes. Old friends. Give me my drink."

"Don't you want to avenge an old friend?"

"It is not my business. Let the police do it."

Barney watched the fisherman's trembling hand grope for the glass. He let Alvarez have it, leaning back in the booth

146

to watch the man with perplexed eyes. Alvarez drank greedily, downing the stuff as if it were water. The juke box stopped playing. Barney got up and put two more nickels in it, preferring the noise to the silence that might carry their voices to the bartender.

When he got back the bottle was almost empty. Alvarez had a glass-eyed expression as Barney slid into the booth again.

"Sol," he said. "I'm counting on you to help me and at the same time, you'll be helping yourself. Of all the men on the *Lucky Q.*, you're the one who has the most reason to want to get even with Peter Hurd. Tell me the truth about what happened on this last trip."

His voice was coaxing and persuasive, but it made no impression on the little fisherman. Barney doubted that Alvarez even saw him. He had made a mistake to let him have the bottle again. He checked his frustration with a sigh. Then suddenly Alvarez began to mumble to himself. At first his words were indistinguishable, then they cleared for a moment.

" — no sense to it, Barney — could

have fixed it up in Osterport — didn't mean to do any harm to anybody — just want my boat — "

"Osterport," Barney said. "Did the *Lucky Q.* put in at Osterport?"

Alvarez looked up. His face was frightened. His dark eyes looked beyond Barney and widened and he gave a little moaning sound and tried to slide out of the booth. His legs tangled with the table supports and he crashed down on the floor, face down. Barney twisted, slewing around as he got up. Chief Petersen stood behind him.

The cop's big face was hard. He wore a blue coat and a gray hat and had a cigar stuck in the corner of his mouth. He took the cigar deliberately from his lips and looked down at the little fisherman who was trying to crawl toward the back door.

"You're getting in my hair, Barney."

Barney said: "I haven't even started. Ask Sol why the *Lucky Q.* put in at Osterport."

"I don't have to ask him nothin'. I got nothin' to do with little Sol. Neither have you."

"Somebody's got to ask these questions, if you don't," Barney said truculently.

"Move," Petersen said. "Make it quick."

Barney studied the big cop's face. For an instant he got the impression that Petersen was trying to give him good advice. Then he decided that Petersen's face told him nothing at all and never would. The cop was an enemy. He was Durand's man. He was only interested in covering up for Durand and Peter Hurd.

Sol Alvarez got to the back door, clawed his way up to the knob, tried to stand up and slid down again on rubbery legs. His face screwed up in childish exasperation and he cursed in fluent Portuguese then Italian. Abruptly, he closed his eyes and went to sleep, sitting with his back against the door.

Petersen said: "Well?"

"I'll be back," Barney told him.

Barney went over to the bar and paid for his ale. The barman said nothing. He went to the door and looked back and saw that Petersen was dragging Alvarez roughly to his feet. He didn't see any reason to interfere.

9

THE car was where he had left it. Barney got in and drove away from the waterfront, up Orient Street to the big house he had once called home and parked in the leaf-littered gravel driveway beside the front porch. It seemed as if all the windows were ablaze with light. Barney crossed the lawn, patted the smooth head of the cast iron deer and went in the front way.

Music drifted down the broad, graceful staircase with its somber, gilt-framed portraits of Barney's seagoing ancestors. He frowned, surprised at the sound that was unusual in this gloomy house and turned to the left to go into the library. Henry was there. He wore a sagging gray turtleneck sweater and old slacks and sneakers. His pale hair was awry and his eyes blazed with anger as he watched Barney come in. His face was hard, uncompromising and his voice trembled.

"It's about time you returned. I've been waiting for you. It's up to you to get them out of here."

Barney lifted a questioning dark brow. "Who are you talking about?"

"Your friends?" Henry snapped. "That trollop who had the nerve to claim she's your fiancée and that slick little man who's your fight manager."

"Lil and Gus?"

"The trollop!" Henry repeated.

"They're here?"

Henry nodded. His fury was just on the verge of bursting out of control. "I won't have them in my house! You understand? I don't care what you do with yourself outside of Easterly, but I won't tolerate them here. Especially not in this house!"

"Take it easy," Barney said. "I'll go see."

He went up the broad stairs two at a time and found Lil readily enough. She was sitting on the edge of the bed in his own bedroom. He was not pleased. He paused, leaning against the door frame and said flatly:

"You look damned comfortable."

Lil looked up and smiled. "I'm making myself at home, lover. You're too hard to keep up with, the way it is. I waited at the gym for you this morning for almost two hours."

"I'll bet. Then what's the idea of this business?"

She wore a tissue thin robe that emphasized the full, firm white flesh of her curved body beneath it. She had been combing her long hair, using a hand mirror and the room smelled heavily of her perfume.

"We're moving in," Lil said throatily. "I told Gus it was silly for us to be staying at the Easterly House and paying for hotel rooms when you've got this big rambling old house and all these empty rooms — "

"It's not my house," Barney interrupted. His dark eyes glinted. "It belongs to Henry."

"Well, what's the difference, anyway? As long as you're going to stay here in Easterly until you fight Reagan, we might as well be cozy, lover."

"Where is Santini?"

"In his room up on the third floor.

152

He said he likes the solitude. He's taking a nap right now, until I call him for dinner. I'm going to do the cooking." Lil stretched out her arms. "Barney, please don't look at me like that. You'll give me the idea you don't love me any more."

"Maybe I don't," he said flatly.

"I thought you forgave me about that money."

"It isn't the money," he said. "It's a lot of things."

She dropped her arms and her eyes hardened. He had never seen quite that expression on her face before. "Things like meeting your old flame again?"

"Maybe," he said.

"Even though she's married to the town's big shot?"

"Maybe," he said again.

"Lover, you're being silly."

"Which room did you choose?" he asked suddenly.

"Right across the hall, darling."

"Then get back to it. Better still, get down to the kitchen and start dinner. If you can cook at all, baby, you'd better make it good. It's going to be tough enough convincing Henry you ought to be allowed to stay."

Lil laughed. "Henry is such a sober-sides."

Barney started to reply, then abruptly closed his mouth and went out of the room. Downstairs, Henry was waiting for him in the library.

"Well?"

"We'd better let them stay," Barney said.

"Not for a minute!"

Barney said: "You want to finish the repairs on the *Mary Hammond*, don't you?"

"What has that got to do with it?" Henry demanded.

"Not much. Only that the money for it came from Gus Santini and there's three thousand more due on the deal. If you want to see the *Mary Hammond* sail again, try to be nice to them, hey?"

He turned and walked out of the house before Henry could reply.

A clean, cold wind scoured the night sky and polished the stars over Easterly. The edge of the moon made a silvery glow on the rim of the sea. Diagonally across the wide, quiet street was the Durand

154

house, a structure of monolithic granite, huge, respectable, dominating the highest point of Orient Street. Barney suddenly remembered Jo's dinner invitation. He didn't think it would be the best policy to go through with it, not only because of Lil and Jo, or the way Henry might act, but because he didn't expect a cordial reception from Mal Durand since their talk in Maria Rodriguez' house. He started across the street, hoping to see Jo and explain and then a car came around the corner and the headlight caught him in their blaze of light. The car swung to the curb beside him.

Jo's voice said: "Hi. I was just coming over to see you."

"I'm sorry," Barney said. "The dinner's off."

"Yes, of course. But I want to talk to you."

"Here on the street?"

"Get in. We'll drive somewhere."

Barney glanced at the stone house, wondering if Durand watched them from one side of the street while Lil watched from the other. He was glad to step into the car and get out of sight of the imaginary, baleful eyes that regarded him.

"Isn't Mal expecting you?" he asked.

"He phoned that he'll be home late." Jo's face was clear and serene in the glow of the dashlights. She handled the big car with ease, turning the corner and rolling downhill toward the highway that led up the Easterly River. "You rather upset him earlier today, I gathered."

"I suppose so," Barney said. "But he asked for it. Where are we going?"

"Wherever you say."

"Let's look at the *Mary Hammond*," he decided.

The river was a placid ribbon of silver under the moonlight as Jo turned into the winding road that led out of town. Barney sat sidewise on the seat, watching Jo's clear profile. He couldn't help comparing her trim, sea-wind beauty with Lil's over-ripe, hothouse lushness. Jo had matured into quite a woman in the past five years. He wondered if Mal Durand knew how lucky he was. He doubted it.

There was very little traffic on the river road. Twice he caught the flash

156

of headlights behind them and their presence stuck like an irritating splinter in the back of his mind. He said: "Jo, did Mal tell you what we talked about?"

"No, he didn't."

"Did he say where we met?"

"No."

"How well does he know Maria Rodriguez?"

Jo was startled. "The widow? He doesn't know her at all."

Barney was silent.

"Well, does he?" Jo asked, her voice troubled.

"I don't know. Turn here, Jo."

They turned off the river road to a dirt road that curved up against a bluff of sandgrown dunes. Barney turned and looked behind them. The headlights that had followed them out of town went on by the turnoff and became twin red tail-lights that swung out of sight after another few moments. The dirt road they were on turned left again, following the crest of the dunes until they came to the shipyard where the *Mary Hammond* had been hauled out on the ways. Two or three floodlights on tall poles illuminated the empty yard and machine shops. Nobody seemed to be about. Jo stopped the car and parked where they could overlook the river and the schooner's hull. Crickets chirped and sang in the tall grass on either side of the road. The wind made the underbrush move restlessly, but the stars and the moon still looked brightly polished, shining and new. The wind was chilly and he put his arm around Jo without thinking too much about it.

"Don't," she whispered.

"I didn't mean anything."

"Things have changed, Barney."

"I know."

"I shouldn't have taken you here."

Barney said: "Because we used to come here after the school dances?" From the car he could look down on the imprisoned schooner and for a moment he had a vision of how she had been a half century ago, dory fishing for cod under topmast canvas. "This is still a nice place."

"It has too many memories," Jo whispered.

"Do you want to forget them, Jo?" he asked.

"I must. It's too late for them now."

She turned toward him suddenly and he saw that her face was tormented. "Barney, why did you have to go away? I loved you so much! You never said anything to me. You treated me as if I were a little nuisance and I probably was, but somehow I always thought that we — that you and I — "

"I was a fool," he said quietly.

"Do you think so — now?"

"I'm sure of it."

"But now it's too late," she whispered.

"I know," he said. "Mal."

"Yes."

"You're not happy with him, Jo?"

"I — I don't know. Not now. I used to think it would be all right — I even thought I loved him and that what I felt for you was just a puppy love affair, an infatuation. But I shouldn't talk like this."

"Go ahead," he said.

"It's just that I'm so worried about you, Barney."

He was surprised. "About me?"

"About you and Mal. He's dangerous. Mal will not tolerate any interference. He can be cruel and ruthless and so coldly brilliant about everything he does that it — it just doesn't seem human."

Barney nodded. "I know."

"Please be careful, Barney."

"Does it matter that much to you, Jo?"

She was silent for a long time. Then she said: "You know it does." When he looked at her again, he saw that she was crying. Her tears were silent, glistening liquid on her smooth cheeks. He didn't know what to do. He felt as if he were being torn apart inside. He wanted to take her in his arms and comfort her, but he knew he couldn't do that, that it wouldn't work, that it was too late, too late for everything.

"Jo," he whispered. "Please."

"It's all right. I'm just a little silly."

"I don't think you're silly at all."

He couldn't help himself. He kissed her. Her lips were warm and wet and salty with her tears. She rubbed her wet cheek against his and came into his arms with a little gasp that was half relief and half dismay. There was a brief moment when her arms clung to him with a strength and desperation he had not suspected in her. Her body trembled in the circle of his arms.

"Jo," he whispered. "Jo, I want you."

"I know." Her voice was almost inaudible, her face buried against his chest. "But there's nothing we can do. I'm sorry about this. I didn't mean to let go and let you see how I feel. I guess I've never been able to keep my emotions hidden from you, have I?"

"I'm glad," he said simply. He felt his control slipping from him fast and elbowed the car door open. "Come on," he said. "Let's walk down and look at the *Mary Hammond*."

She agreed mutely, recognizing the pitfall that yawned before them. Hand in hand, they followed the footpath down toward the marine railways below. The floodlights made odd pools of brightness here and there among the sheds and machine shops, casting long, distorted shadows of equipment before them. No one challenged them as they went through the open gate and approached the cradle of oak timbers where the schooner rested. Barney paused and studied Henry's fishing boat. He wanted to get Jo out of his mind and he turned his thoughts to the other night when an old man had died with a knife in him — died in hate and a burning, suicidal drive toward revenge. He frowned, thinking about it. Everything he had done and learned today had simply enlarged the problem, opening new corridors of darkness that angled off in different directions, leaving him perplexed and unable to choose the right one.

Barney turned and looked back at the little watchman's shack they had passed. Old Sam Jones must be sound asleep, he thought, to leave everything unguarded like this. A little nagging imp of worry and uneasiness touched the edge of his mind.

"Let's go back," Jo said. "We shouldn't be here."

"In a minute."

"Mal will be wondering — "

"To hell with Mal," he said savagely. "Don't worry about him."

Her face was pale and serious. "Barney, we have to understand each other. Mal is my husband. I married him in good faith. Things haven't worked out the way I hoped they would, but perhaps it's as much my fault as his. I don't want you and Mal to be enemies."

He laughed harshly. "Jo, what else could we be?"

"I don't know. But I'm frightened. I have a terrible feeling that you and Mal — "

She had no chance to finish what she was going to say. The high, sharp, vicious report of a rifle slapped across her words. The sound of it echoed back and forth from the hills and dunes that edged the silvery river. Barney stared at a spurt of sand that suddenly jumped at his feet. Jo looked at him, her mouth open. Before she could speak, the rifle cracked again. This time Barney felt the quick whipcrack of air as the bullet went by his head and slapped into the oak planking of the schooner that towered behind them.

"Get down!" he yelled.

He pushed Jo headlong into the deep shadows under the curving hull, and flung himself after her, half covering her with his body. A third bullet glanced off the copper bottom sheathing of the massive hull and whined away across the moonlit river.

"Barney, what — "

"Keep quiet," he said harshly.

They were momentarily protected by the shadows under the schooner. The echoes of the last rifle shot died away and there were no more. Everything looked the same. Nothing had changed. Moonlight dappled the shipyard while the silent pools of brilliance from the overhead floodlights remained unchanged and mute. Nothing stirred within the range of his vision. He searched higher, back to the path that led up the hill to the dirt road where they had parked the car. There was nothing to see. But someone was out there. Someone with a rilfe, someone with murder in his heart.

Barney shivered.

He looked at the watchman's shack, but there was no sign of the old man who usually guarded the shipyard at night. A car went by on the upper highway with a rush and flare of headlights. Jo gripped his hand. Her fingers were cold and trembling.

"Who was it, Barney? Can you see?"

"I don't know," he whispered.

"Can we get out of here?"

He didn't reply. He kept searching the dark pattern of silver and shadows in the low dunes and hills. Nobody had come through the gate where they had entered. He remembered the car that had followed them out of town and knew that he had been badly tricked. Anger rose in him. And exultation. Apparently he had touched a raw nerve somwhere, in somebody, with the questions he had asked during the day. He felt no fear for himself. His only anxiety was for Jo.

The pressure of the big hull balanced over their heads was enormous, a psychological trap that added to Jo's trembling. It would be easy to slip under the boat and escape through the shadows on the other side in order to work their way back to the parked car. But he didn't want to escape. He itched with a fury to get his hands on the man up there with the rifle.

And then he saw him.

It was just a flicker of movement on the side of the grassgrown dune, a movement that couldn't have been caused by the wind or the underbrush. It came and went, catching his eye with a metallic glint of moonlight on a rifle barrel. Barney let out his breath in a long sigh.

"Stay here, Jo."

"No," she said quickly. "I want to go with you."

"Please."

He got up quickly before she could argue and sprinted across the hard, gravelly sand toward the watchman's shack. For a space of seconds he had to cross in front of one of the glaring floodlights. He heard the rifle crack and sand spurted in a spray at his feet and Jo screamed, a tight sound against the silver and velvet night. He dived headlong again into the shadows behind the watchman's shack and sprawled motionless in the sand. His blood pumped crazily inside his head. Carefully he raised his head and scanned the dark dunes before him. He was about a hundred yards from where he had glimpsed moonlight on the rifle barrel. He drew another deep breath and crawled up to the watchman's window and looked inside. Nobody was in there. He knew that old Sam Jones carried a gun, an old Smith & Wesson .38, and he had a vague hope he might find it in here. But it wasn't within ready sight and he had no time to go inside and look for it. He glanced back toward the schooner's hull, looking for Jo, but she wasn't to be seen. Gathering himself, he got up and ran again, racing for the shipyard gate.

The rifle cracked once more before he reached the deep shadow of the sand dune. Five misses, he thought. He was lucky, or else the man with the gun was an awfully poor shot. His fragmentary thoughts rejected this, touched with puzzlement and then he stopped thinking and allowed his animal senses to take over while he stalked his quarry.

The underbrush and wild beach plums suddenly rattled and a thin shower of sand and gravel rolled down the dune toward him. A man's figure was silhouetted against the sky for an instant, rifle in hand. Barney got up and plunged up the dune toward him. The man yelled in sudden alarm and vanished toward the dirt path that Barney and Jo had taken only a few minutes before. The soft sand and gravel yielded underfoot, offering only a treacherous grip as Barney tried to scramble after the shadowy figure. He reached the top of the dune and dropped flat, careful not to give his enemy a clear silhouette against the moonlit sky. Cautiously he searched the terrain ahead of him.

He saw nothing. Crickets chirped and sang and from far up the river came the distant, muted tolling of a bell buoy. Nothing moved. The pattern of black and silver was undisturbed.

He waited, listening. But his opponent obviously was playing the same game and it was Barney who was under pressure, worried lest Jo come up here after him before it was safe. It was up to Barney to make the next move. He dried the sweat off his palms on his thighs. Before him there was a little dip and then the rise to the next dune along the crest of which ran the dirt road where they had parked the car. The valley directly ahead was in deep shadow. Barney sidled to the left, keeping just below the ridge of his dune and then got up and charged down into the dark shadows.

In the instant when the man rose up before him, directly in his path, he knew that he had misjudged the matter badly. He had thought the man with the rifle had retreated to the road. Instead, he had waited on the opposite side of the dune for Barney's rush. He only had time to glimpse the dark outline of the man and see the quick swing of the rifle butt before it crashed down on his head.

The night exploded in a shower of bright lights and screaming pain. He went down, his face plowing a furrow in the coarse sand. The earth heaved and spun under him. He tried to get up again and rose on hands and knees but couldn't lift himself further. Footsteps grated in the coarse ground, running away from him. He thought he heard Jo's voice calling to him, but he didn't turn around to look for her. Somewhere a car motor started up, roared as the engine was raced and then throbbed away. Lights flared beyond the ridge of the dune. Tail-lights winked, jeering at him.

Jo came running up to where he crouched on hands and knees. Her face was anguished.

"Barney! Barney, are you all right?"

Her hands sought him, her arms supported him as he rose staggering to his feet. For several more moments the world kept spinning in nauseating circles around him. Then Jo's face cleared before his eyes and he managed a lopsided grin.

"Yeah. Yeah, I'm great. Good and stupid. I let him clobber me but good."

"As long as you're safe," she whispered. She was trembling violently. "Let's get out of here."

"Fine with me," he muttered. Then he lifted his head again. "Funny thing — he could have clubbed me to death, but he didn't. He had the chance. And the car he was using, did you see it?"

"No," Jo said. "What does it matter?"

"It was my car," he told her. "The bastard used the Ford that Gus Santini loaned me."

10

HE dreamed the same dream every night in the week that followed. He was running down a blind alley that came to a dead end. When he came to the blank wall that barred his way, he tried to gauge the distance to the top and jump for it, but no matter how hard he tried, how strong or high he jumped, the top of the wall was always just a little beyond his scrambling fingers. He fell back exhausted time and again and when he was thoroughly spent, someone up there, a figure of darkness without a face or a name, laughed at him and threw something out over him that settled like a net around his struggling figure. The more he fought to get out of the net, the more tightly he became enmeshed in its strands.

Once, on the third night after the shipyard affair, he awoke to find Lil Ollander in his room. It was another moonlit night and her figure was only too clearly defined by the light that came in through the open window.

"Lover, what's the matter?"

He sat up in the bed, confused. "Nothing," he said. "I had a dream, that's all."

"You were yelling as if you were being killed."

He looked at her more closely. Her negligee was nothing that mattered. Under it, her body looked white and curved and creamy.

"You'd better go back to your own bed, Lil."

She smiled and came toward him instead, sitting down beside him. Her hands moved through his dark, rumpled hair. He couldn't read the enigmatic expression in her eyes. Her perfume touched him and wrapped itself around him in subtle, sinuous strands. It reminded him of the net in his dreams.

"Lover, don't you want me any more?"

"I'm in training," he said.

She laughed. "Don't try to fool me, lover. Nothing's been the same since you came up here."

"You'll wake up Henry," he said.

172

"I don't care. He's weird. He hates me, doesn't he?"

"He doesn't approve of you," Barney replied. Lil was leaning over him, leaving nothing to his imagination. His hands ached. He thought of Jo, asleep somewhere with Mal Durand in the big house across the street. He wanted to yell and strike out at something, at anybody, in his frustration. He controlled his voice. "It's still Henry's house. Don't do anything to upset him, Lil."

"You worry too much about him and not enough about me, lover," Lil whispered huskily. She looked sleepy and sensuous in the cool moonlight. Her lips were full and pouting. She looked down at him and laughed softly, a thick and seductive sound, full of honey and cream that bubbled deep in her smooth throat. "You know you want me, darling."

Barney moved quickly, recognizing his own weakness. He slid out of bed on the opposite side, came around toward the girl and scooped her up in his arms. She giggled softly. The sound of her amusement died abruptly as he carried her to the hall door, kicked it open and dropped her unceremoniously to her feet out there.

"And stay out, baby," he said grimly.

He shut the door on the soft, slurring sound of her angry vituperation, grinned, rubbed a hand over his face and thoughtfully turned the lock against her return. He knew she would never forgive him for her injured pride now, but that didn't matter. Lil was a mistake that he had outgrown. He went to the window and stared out over the moonlit harbor town. His thoughts drifted back to the repetitive dream that had awakened him.

Dead end.

It was as if the attack on him at the shipyard had been a kind of final curtain dropping down before him, blocking all the questions he had asked during the past few days. Nothing more happened. He went to Carlos DeFalgia's funeral with Henry and they were the only people there until Jo arrived. When he went back to Maria Rodriguez' house, the place was locked and empty and there was no reply to his repeated knocking. No one knew if the woman had left town or whether she had simply gone into seclusion. Even Tal Carter down at the Town Landing became a clam with no answers.

Chief Petersen announced to the press that the investigation was proceeding along routine lines and that any new developments would be divulged promptly. But there were no new developments. When Barney tried to look up Sol Alvarez, he was told that the former owner of the *Lucky Q.* had gone to Provincetown to visit relatives.

Dead end.

The weather held fair through the end of September. He worked out regularly at the Y gym every morning, did road work in the afternoon. His body felt tuned to a fine, sharp edge. He felt confident about the coming fight with Tony Reagan. But there was a difference in other respects. He had lived and breathed the fight game for five years, drawing zest and enthusiasm from each new bout that carried him upward along the ladder toward the championship. Now the championship seemed relatively unimportant to him. He couldn't explain the change in his attitude. Gus Santini noticed it and worried about it, but Barney put him off with a grunt and a reminder to be sure to place the remaining three thousand dollars with a trustworthy gambler. Santini assured him that this would be done and continued to worry about Barney's lack of enthusiasm for the fight with Reagan. Santini told him that he had intervened with the boxing commission and after the fight he would be allowed to go back to New York, his fight career insured. Barney accepted the news without caring much either way.

* * *

You never know, Barney thought. You string along with a smooth operator like Gus Santini for all these years and your life turns upside down. The Broadway Kid, Barney Hammond, contender for the middleweight championship, on top of the heap, climbing all over the suckers. The lights and sweet music and all the girls in the world. Lil Ollander. Swell apartments, a kaleidoscope of arenas, red gloves, sweat, the sting of ammonia, the smell of resin, the clang of bells marking off the rounds, the months and the years. Like a guy with puppets, Barney thought. That was Gus Santini. Staging everything, waiting. And building him up for the kill.

Gus Santini drove him down to Boston for the fight with Reagan. They went alone, just the two of them, slipping out of town in the early hours of morning and Lil didn't come along. Henry was already at the shipyard watching the work on the *Mary Hammond* with a brooding, jealous eye. Lil would join them later, Gus said. She would come down by train.

He slept through the afternoon in a hotel room near the Commons while Gus took care of reporters and hangers-on and arranged for handlers. Gus was good at taking care of the details. Barney said nothing about the smooth, dark-faced man who kept slipping in to whisper to Santini. Money changed hands. Barney saw it and rolled over to sleep some more.

When he awoke again, the room was growing shadowed and Gus was sitting in a chair by the window, smoking a cigar. They were alone.

"Where is Lil?" Barney asked, sitting up.

"She hasn't shown up yet. Don't worry about her," Gus looked concerned. "This Tony Reagan has a right like a bomb, Barney. He likes to cut up around the eyes. You want to watch out for that."

"He won't touch me," Barney said.

He got dressed, wondering why Gus Santini looked so worried. Uneasiness squirmed inside him. He wondered if Gus was planning to pull another fast one. He watched the slickhaired man go to the telephone and call the North Station, checking on the arrival of trains from Easterly. He hung up, chewing the corner of his mouth.

"She should have been here by now," Gus said.

"Lil?"

"An hour ago," Santini said.

"She'll be here," Barney nodded.

"She'd better be."

Barney looked up sharply at the tension in Santini's voice. "There's something more important than Lil right now,

Gus. I've got three grand more coming to me."

"I know, Barney. I know."

"Before the fight."

"Listen, Barney — "

"Three grand or Al Koch's slip. The odds are two to one for Reagan." Al Koch was the gambler Santini usually dealt with. "Have you got Al's slip?"

Santini's face was pale. "Barney, Lil has it."

"What?"

"She took the money. She said she'd take care of everything." Santini backed away as Barney stood up. "Kid, listen to me. Believe me. I wouldn't try to pull anything funny on you. Not any more. You taught me my lesson, and I held no grudges against you. Honest! Listen, kid, she'll show up any minute. Something's delayed her, that's all! There's nothing to worry about!"

"Gus, I'll kill you," Barney's voice grated in the hotel room. He was trembling with anger. "If you've crossed me again, so help me, I won't stop until you — "

"Please, Barney." Gus looked genuinely

frightened. "I'll make it good out of my own pocket if she doesn't show up."

"Now," Barney said.

"I don't have any money like that with me — "

"Now!" Barney repeated.

He moved toward the fight manager. He wanted to kill the little man. He knew what had happened. Lil had not forgotten the night he had thrown her out of his room. She had read the handwriting on the wall, writing he had made as plain to her as possible. He was through with her, and her vindictive nature had taken this way to exact her revenge. She wasn't in Easterly. She might be in Boston right now, but he'd never see her. She would be watching the fight somewhere, laughing at him, his money in her purse.

The question that remained was whether Gus Santini had played her game for her, knowing what she planned. He turned away from Santini and heard the man's audible sigh of relief. Using the room phone, he put through a call to Easterly and asked the operator for Henry's number.

The telephone rang for a long time. He could visualize it ringing in that big, empty, lonely house on Orient Street. Nobody answered it. He hung up, canceled the call.

"She isn't there, Gus."

Santini stopped trying to sidle toward the door. His face was ashen. He held up both hands, palms up, in a defensive gesture.

"Barney, I swear to you — she said you told her to put the three grand down on you to win. With Al Koch, like you always do. I heard her talk to Al on the phone yesterday, Barney!"

Barney's eyes glistened. "When yesterday?"

"Just before dinner, kid."

"And she put the bet down for me?"

"I heard her tell Al she'd bring the money with her from Easterly. She was supposed to stop there between the railroad station and coming here, Barney."

Barney snapped a thumb toward the telephone. "Call Al."

"Now?"

"Call him."

181

Santini got the number after a few moment's delay. Barney paced the floor, his face dark with anger, his body tense like a caged animal's. He listened to Santini's stumbling words when he talked to the New York gambler. He hung up and shook his head.

"She ain't been there yet. But she'll show, Barney — "

She was laughing at him somewhere here in town, he thought. She'd played him for a sucker all these years, milking him out of the money he'd earned with a hearts-and-flowers vision of the future. How dumb could a guy get? He wondered. He looked at Santini. The little man seemed to shrink visibly away from his gaze. There was no way of being sure. Not right now. He had a fight to take care of, with Tony Reagan . . .

His anger carried with him to the Arena, down into the dressing room. He tried to call Easterly again and again there was no answer to the lonely ringing telephone. And Lil didn't turn up.

His face was a blank mask as he came down the aisle and slid under the ropes into the ring. Tony Reagan was a squat, flat-faced boy with calm, dangerous eyes. The crowd liked him. For one of the few times in Barney's career, he was not the favorite to win. Which would have been just great if he hadn't been such a sucker for the oldest double-crossing game in the world.

He had his hands full the moment the bell rang. Tony Reagan came out of his corner in a fast crouch, his gloves stabbing continuously. He was fast, tricky and confident. His teeth glistened in a momentary grin as Barney tried a long right that slid harmlessly over his shoulder. He bore in with two quick lefts that pounded Barney's middle and brought a roar from the South Boston crowd. Barney back-peddled, his eyes wary.

There came a flurry of gloves, leather thudding on flesh. Barney paid off with short, stabbing lefts. His thick black hair looped wetly over his forehead. His back grazed the ropes and he moved sidewise as if shocked. Tony Reagan feinted, then suddenly stabbed at Barney's eye. Lights exploded inside Barney's head, as if a red-hot poker had been slammed across his brow. The crowd roared. He grabbed desperately for the ropes, felt his body bounce against the referee, swung away and fell into a clinch. He jabbed with his left, broke free and swung with his right. Reagan went inside the blow, taking it easily on his shoulder and ripped a left to Barney's middle then a stabbing right to Barney's eye again. The crowd howled as the bell rang.

He tried to spot Lil in the blur of faces surrounding the ring. He didn't see her. The handler Gus had hired babbled in his ear and Santini shouted up something from the dirty floor behind his corner. He didn't pay any attention.

The second round went worse than the first. You couldn't have your mind on anything else and expect to take someone like this Reagan boy, no matter how much ring savvy you have. Reagan was good, he was anxious to win. His gloves were a swift blur before Barney's cautious defense. He caught Barney's eye again within a matter of seconds, but he paid attention to Barney's ribs now, too.

Barney covered up, waiting and watching for his chance.

He managed to land a lucky punch that bounced off Reagan's jaw and the South Boston boy staggered for a moment. Barney thought, *It's now or never*, and wound up with a long right. He took too much time; the punch was telegraphed. When it was halfway gone he knew he was still underestimating his opponent. Barney never saw the bombshell that caught him on the side of the head. It exploded hard and sure and Barney's knees gave way.

He lay face down, hearing the crowd bellow beyond the ropes. The referee counted over him.

" . . . three — four — five — "

He got to his feet at eight. The referee wiped his gloves and ducked away and Tony Reagan danced in, just as the bell ended the round.

Fighting wasn't the same any more. He remembered Peter Hurd and the two old fishermen, both dead and his brother Henry's anxious, worried face. He thought of Jo. He had half hoped she might be here tonight, but now he was glad that she wasn't. He didn't want her to see his last fight. Abruptly his thinking ended in a wave of bitter anger.

Gus Santini's voice came up from the ringside, soft and anxious.

"Barney, listen — don't disappoint me."

Barney grinned and let the handler pop his mouth-guard over his teeth. "Who did you put your money on, Gus?"

"You, Barney. You."

"To hell with you, Gus."

"You said you could take this Reagan boy, Barney!"

"I'll take him," Barney said. "But not for you."

He was on his feet and moving fast when the bell rang for the third round. It was the Broadway Kid in the ring suddenly and the crowd somehow sensed it. So did Tony Reagan. The squat boy's confident jabs were knocked down as Barney danced and feinted and drove him back to the ropes. Reagan looked puzzled. Barney landed a left to the jaw and Reagan sagged into a clinch.

Barney slid deftly to one side. He connected with a hard right jab and Reagan dropped to one knee, came up clawing the air. Barney's ring knowledge, suddenly awakened, had turned him into a lethal fighter. He grinned at Reagan's confusion. Everything faded away but the instinct to hit hard and true. Overhead, the lights glared in baleful brilliance through the writhing smoke and the crowd noises made a tangible curtain that closed him in, shutting out the rest of the world while he hammered away at the target.

The end came just before the bell. Reagan tried a last-chance hook that Barney rolled aside on his shoulder. And Barney came up under the other's guard. His right crossed swiftly, the red glove made a sharp cracking sound of leather on bone. The crowd screamed like a frenzied animal. Reagan dropped to the deck, flat on his back, arms outflung. His chest heaved, but he didn't move. The referee's hands were on Barney, shoving him back into a neutral corner, then he began his count. Barney leaned his elbows on the rope, breathing deep gulps of the thick, strangling air. His body was covered with a light, cool sweat. He saw the referee come toward him, waving his arms and then his glove was lifted and he heard the booming announcement through the loudspeakers, disembodied beyond the noise of the crowd. Barney lifted a glove to the crowd and ducked under the ropes, surrounded by the sweatshirted handlers who hurried to keep up with his swift pace back to the dressing room.

Gus Santini was jubilant.

"I knew you could do it, Barney! You're better than ever. You'll go right to the top again."

"You still owe me three grand," Barney said shortly.

"But Lil — "

"Lil isn't here. The three grand, Gus."

"All right, Barney. It's yours."

The dressing room was a madhouse. "Now," Barney said.

"Sure thing."

Gus turned his back on the crowd and jammed a roll of bills into Barney's clothing that hung in the locker. His face was pale, shining with sweat. His black eyes shone with bright anger for a moment.

"Satisfied?"

Barney grinned. "You sure you haven't heard anything from Lil?"

"No, Barney."

11

GUS herded most of the reporters and congratulatory fans out of the dressing room. Barney hurried through the rubdown and shower. "See if you can find Al Koch," he said.

Gus rushed out the door to locate the gambler before he left. Barney dressed carefully, feeling the weariness in his body, the slow spread of aches and bruises. He had won, but it didn't mean anything. He felt none of the exultation in triumph that he used to experience. One of the handlers put a piece of white court plaster over his right eye.

"You were great, kid," the man said. "You're gonna be champ."

"No," Barney said. "This is my last fight."

"What?"

"Beat it," Barney said. "Out."

The handler made a quick exit, heading for the sports writers with his headline. Al Koch came in followed by Gus Santini. Barney knotted his necktie and regarded the little gambler evenly.

"Al," he said. "I want you to play it straight for me."

Koch grinned. "You made me lose a bundle tonight, kid. But I've got no grief against you. You're a fighter. Next time I'll know better."

"There won't be any next time," Barney said. He went on over their protests, "What I want to know is about my dough."

"You should have had something down on yourself, kid."

"I thought I did."

Koch shook his head. "Nobody got in touch with me on it."

"You're sure of that?"

"Of course I'm sure."

"You didn't hear from Lil Ollander?"

"Not a word." He paused. "That is, not since last night."

Barney was satisfied. Koch was as honest and straight as they came. Gus Santini wanted to know what he meant by saying this was his last time. Barney didn't bother to reply.

"Give me the keys to your car, Gus," he said.

"What for? Where are you going?"

"Back to Easterly — to find Lil."

"Barney, she won't be there any more. If she's got your dough, she's making quick tracks with it by now."

"I'll find her," Barney said. "I'll start in Easterly."

"Barney, keep your head. Don't do anything crazy."

"I'd like to kill her," Barney grated.

Gus looked scared. "Kid — "

"Shut up!" Barney said. "Give me the car keys."

Gus gave them to him. He left the Arena by the back gates, avoiding the crowd and walked through the dark street to the parking lot where Santini had left his convertible. The air felt cold and raw and there were no stars over South Boston. It felt as if it was going to rain.

There was a telephone in the attendant's booth at the back of the lot. Barney gave the man a dollar and put through another call to Easterly. Maybe Henry would know something about Lil's disappearance.

He felt a dark rage overspreading his mind and watched his hands shake as he held the telephone. The fight with Tony Reagan was already in the dead past, done and forgotten. It was his last fight. He was through with the rotten, doublecrossing racket. If Gus Santini was a part of Lil's plan to do him out of his money, he would find that out and follow the little man to the ends of the earth for his revenge.

The telephone began to ring in the house on Orient Street.

It rang again and again. There was no answer. Barney looked at his watch, saw it was only a few minutes after ten o'clock. Uneasiness spread through him as he listened to the lonely ringing of the telephone. He told himself there was no reason why Henry had to be at home at this hour. Henry could be anywhere. But he would know something about Lil anyway, give him enough to start him on the chase after the doublecrossing bitch.

The operator said: "I'm sorry. Shall I try again in twenty minutes?"

"Cancel it," Barney said.

He hung up savagely. The parking lot

attendant had Gus's car ready for him.

It began to rain when he was still half an hour from Easterly. It was after eleven by then. The rain came down in big, slow drops at first, spattering the windshield, blackening the road. Then it thickened, sluicing down in wind driven sheets that wavered like ghosts in the glare of the headlights. It hammered the canvas top of the car, leaked in through the windwing. Barney didn't slacken speed until the first glimmering lights of Easterly showed up ahead.

"The bitch," he muttered.

I ought to kill her, he thought.

He swung across the Town Landing, skidding on the wet cobblestones and turned uphill toward Orient Street. Durand's house was in total darkness except for a dim glow of light from one room deep in the interior. Barney parked the car by the sidewalk and got out into the rain to stare at his own house. It looked perfectly normal in the darkness. One upstairs window was lighted and one on the main floor. The rain slackened somewhat as he pushed through the iron gate and crossed the lawn to the front door.

It wasn't locked. He stepped inside, wiped water from his wet face and paused in the central hallway.

"Henry!" he called.

His voice went echoing up the wide, gracefully curved staircase and was lost in the emptiness of the big house. The solemn dark portraits of his ancestors frowned down at him in silence. He turned on his heel, threw open the library doors and looked inside. Nobody was here. His anger slackened a little. The house felt cold and damp and he shivered a little and headed into the kitchen, putting on the lights as he went. He found a bottle of old Jamaica rum and poured himself a stiff drink in a water tumbler. It didn't stop his shivering.

He poured himself another drink and listened to the rain beating against the windows. There was no reason for him to feel this queer uneasiness, he thought. Lil was gone, of course, and Henry was simply out somewhere on his own business. He began to wonder if he had gone off half-cocked again, driving back here like this. Then he thought he heard the sound of a soft footfall upstairs. He slammed down the drink of rum and strode back to the hallway again.

"Henry?" he called.

The rain mocked him with its soft whispering.

"Lil?"

Something bothered him. He didn't know what it was. There was an elusive feeling that something was missing, wrong, or out of place in the hallway. He looked around at the portraits of his grandfather and great grandfather. Their stern, forbidding faces told him nothing. Near the library door was a wide mahogany panel on which were mounted an assortment of fishing rigs, old harpoons from the dorying days. Barney stared at the panel and suddenly realized what was troubling him.

One of the sharp, barbed harpoons was missing.

He went up the staircase quickly and quietly. The upper hallway was dark. He didn't put on the light. He went toward the back room where Henry slept and there was a harsh, acrid taste of fear in the back of his mouth. Henry's room was dark, too. The bed was neatly made, everything scrupulously tidy. Henry wasn't there.

When he turned back, he noticed for the first time a thin bar of light that seeped under the door to the room Lil had been using.

He didn't want to open the door. He wanted to back down the stairs, to get out of the house and run. His legs told him to run, to forget about Lil's room, to forget about the whole thing and just get out of there.

He opened the door and looked inside.

A dim lamp shone beside the big fourposter bed. The shade was pink and it seemed to bathe the whole room in its ruddy glow. Everything seemed normal. The room was empty. The big bed disheveled, as if Lil hadn't bothered to straighten up in her hurry to make her getaway this morning. Barney let out a long breath and felt the trembling slowly leave him. One of the windows near the bed was still open several inches and he walked over to close it, his gesture automatic, unthinking.

He almost stepped on the harpoon on

the other side of the bed.

He looked down at it and felt the yell rise unbidden to his throat, a sound of panic and horror. Lil sprawled on the carpeted floor beside the bed, as if she had slid out of it on her back. She was only half dressed and what remained of her clothing was ripped and torn as if she had been attacked by a wild animal, baring the rich fullness of her body. Her mouth was open and her eyes stared in wild terror at Barney as he bent over her.

The harpoon had been planted with a deep and savage thrust into the middle of her chest, between her breasts.

He didn't have to look at her twice to know that she was dead. She had been dead for a long time, for most of the day. The blood from the wound was thickly clotted, the dark rivulets frozen across the creamy whiteness of her ribs.

He began to shake. He couldn't help himself. It was senseless, a crazy, brutal thing that had nothing to do with what had happened here before. There could be no connection between Lil and the old DeFalgia brothers. She was supposed to have been a hundred miles from here with Barney's three thousand dollars. She was supposed to be laughing at him because she had played him for a sucker once more. But she wasn't laughing. She was dead. Someone had come in here, surprised her, fought with her and driven that sharp, barbed harpoon deep into her body while she stared at her murderer in paralyzed terror.

Senseless.

He listened to the rain tapping against the glass. Some of it had spattered over the sill of the window that was partly open and made a little pool of glistening water on the polished floor. Barney backed away toward the bedroom door. He couldn't stop shaking. He wanted to run, but he knew that if he ran he would be lost forever.

Movement stirred the dark hallway behind him. Too late he remembered the sound of that footfall that had first brought him up here. He started to turn, saw a faint glimmer of ruddy light reflected on something bright and shining and then pain crashed down through his head, driving him to his knees and a glaring light exploded all around him. He heard the sound of a scream and he thought it was Lil's voice. But Lil was dead and maybe it was he who was screaming.

Then the darkness folded quietly around him and he didn't think about anything for a long time.

12

THE first voice said: "Let him lay."

The second one said: "Hell, it ain't decent, Charley."

"We'll wait for the pix."

"Even so, Charley — "

The first voice said: "Ah, shut up. It'll make a pretty picture, won't it?"

The voices seemed to come from a long way off, as if through a long, dark tunnel. The words became garbled, bouncing back and forth inside his head. Barney tried to understand the rest of what they were saying, but he couldn't make it out and after a little while he gave up trying. He wondered what had happened to him. The back of his head ached. When he opened his eyes, he saw nothing but a vague, gray darkness. Terror touched him. He thought he was blind. He tried to move, to sit up and found that his hand was holding something hard and cylindrical and the rest of his arm rested on something smooth and cold. He pulled his hand away in a gesture of sudden fright and sat up. His head almost came off in a quick pulse of pain that tore through him down to his stomach. He was almost sick. He fought down the rising nausea and sat up.

He had been holding the shaft of the harpoon, one arm outflung over Lil Ollander's naked, dead body. Everything came back to him. He looked around and saw two pairs of trousered legs standing in front of him. He looked up higher and saw that they belonged to two cops, who were watching him with morbid interest.

"Awake now, Barney?" one of them asked.

"Leave him alone, Charley," said the second one.

"Hell, we ought to give the son-of-a-bitch what he rates."

Barney got up slowly. Neither of the two uniformed cops touched him or offered to help. The room swam dizzily around him and he had to hold on to one of the bedposts to steady himself. He looked down at Lil's body and then looked at his hand. It was trembling like a leaf in the wind. Somehow he found his voice.

"What's this all about?"

"Suppose you tell us, Barney."

"I don't know anything about it — "

The first cop laughed. The sound was obscene in that room. "Look, kid, we come here and find you out cold on top of the dame — "

"Somebody slugged me," Barney said. "Where is Henry?"

"We're looking for him."

"Didn't you find anybody else?"

"Just you and the dame. Why'd you kill her like that?"

"I didn't," Barney said.

The first cop looked pleased. "You're gonna make this real interesting for us. It's gonna be a real pleasure, beatin' the truth out of you. Nobody else was here in this house except you and the girl. You rammed the harpoon into her and stumbled and knocked yourself out on the bedpost. Or don't you remember?"

"It didn't happen that way," Barney said. "How come you cops got here like this?"

"Your fight manager, Mr. Santini, telephoned the chief from Boston," the first cop said. He was a big, blunt-faced man with a thick voice that relished every word he spoke. "Your manager said you were heading back to Easterly with murder in your eye. The dame here doublecrossed you and swiped three thousand dollars that she was supposed to be holding for you. Mr. Santini said you talked and acted crazy and he was worried in case you caught up to the dame and did something to her you'd regret. I guess he called us a little too late."

Barney sat down on the edge of the bed, opposite from where Lil sprawled in death. His head ached. He understood a little of what the cop was saying but not all of it. Enough to know that he was in trouble, deep trouble and there was no easy way out of it. His stomach turned and twisted inside him and again he thought he was going to be sick. He didn't want to be sick in front of these cops. He fought down the nausea once more and licked his dry lips.

"You've got it all wrong," he whispered. "I didn't kill her."

"Like I say," said the first cop grinning, "it's going to be a pleasure to beat the truth out of you."

"Stay away from me," Barney warned.

"Hell, you're reserved for Chief Petersen. He gets first crack at you. He's going to enjoy it, too. He'll be along any minute."

Barney struggled to gather his wits. "Look, I was in Boston all day. Maybe you heard the fight on the radio."

The second cop, a small man with a sharp, alert face and intelligent eyes nodded. "We listened to it. It was a good fight."

"All right," Barney said. "This girl has been dead for a good many hours. The body's cold. How could I have done this if I was out of town all day?"

The first cop said heavily: "Maybe you came back and done it. Was somebody with you all the time you was in Boston?"

"Of course," Barney said.

"We can check on it, mister. The fact that you think you're a big shot don't cut ice with me. We'll check on every minute of your time today and check it good."

Barney was aware of a sinking sensation

as his mind swung back through the last few hours. He had slept most of the afternoon away in the hotel room and Gus Santini had been with him throughout that time. Or had he? Gus could have come and gone half a dozen times and Barney hadn't awakened to notice his absence. Suppose Gus went out for a couple of hours or more? Theoretically, that would have given him time to drive back here, kill Lil and get back to the hotel and feign sleep again. It was just barely possible. But it was thin and nobody in his right mind would believe it.

He chewed his lip thoughtfully, wishing his head didn't ache so much. Suppose Gus Santini was sore about the way he forced him to part with another three grand? Barney suddenly slapped his back pocket and took out his wallet. The cops watched him in silence. He counted the money and put it away, ignoring them. It was all there. And suppose Gus said he *could* have come back and killed Lil? He'd shot off his mouth plenty about what he'd like to do to her — he'd even said he wanted to kill her. It had just been his temper, but with the girl dead, everything he had said and done took on a new meaning. If the cops wanted to believe him guilty, they could. He swallowed, tasting panic in the back of his throat.

"Let me wash up?" he asked the cops.

"You stay right where you are," said Charley.

The smaller cop said quietly: "I'll go with him. Come on, fella."

Barney moved carefully out of the room to the bath at the end of the hall. The house was quiet. The rain tapped on the windows in dull and monotonous rhythm. He washed the back of his head where blood was already clotting and scrubbed his hands hard as if he could get the feel of the smooth harpoon shaft from his fingers. When he was finished, the smaller cop lit two cigarettes and handed Barney one of them. He had a dark, thin face that looked vaguely familiar. Barney asked him his name.

"Fred Alvarez," the cop said.

"Sol's brother?"

The cop nodded. "We were partners

until we lost the *Lucky Q*."

"Is Sol all right?"

"He's in the hospital."

"What happened?"

The little cop shrugged. "He was drunk. He tangled with some characters on the waterfront. Nobody knows who it was. He's got a busted hand and three cracked ribs and his nose is split."

Barney felt a cold horror inside him. "He was talking to me about Hurd," he said.

"I know that."

"But he didn't tell me anything," Barney said.

"Hurd doesn't know that."

"Then you think Hurd did it to Sol?"

The little cop shrugged again. "I'm sure of it."

"And you don't do anything about it?"

"I've thought of something," the cop said.

He didn't go any further with it. Barney dragged deeply at the cigarette. He sensed a friendliness in the little cop that he didn't want to push too hard or too fast. The cigarette smoke felt good in his lungs. Somewhere in the town the sound of a siren lifted in the wet night. It wailed away and came up again, drawing nearer. Fred Alvarez went to the bathroom door and called something to Charley and footsteps went clattering down the front stairs. The little cop turned and looked at Barney with speculative eyes.

"We've got a couple of minutes," he said. "Maybe less. If you've got anything to say, spill it out now, quick."

"What's there to say?" Barney asked. "I didn't kill her. Anybody with half a grain of sense would know that."

"Sure. But Petersen's going to jump all over you." The little cop looked bitter. "Nothing's done right in this town since Durand made Petersen the chief. Hell, I've only been a cop since Sol and me lost our boat, but it's easy to smell the rotten fish buried under Town Hall." The little cop stabbed at Barney with his voice. "Do you think this girl's death was tied up with the old DeFalgia brothers' murders?"

"I don't know," Barney said truthfully. "I don't see how it could be."

209

"Maybe she learned something. Did you have anything in this house that she could have gotten hold of and tried to use for herself — some information she thought she could trade for money?"

"No," Barney said. "Nothing."

"There has to be a reason for it, if you didn't kill her."

"I didn't," Barney said.

"Then it's got to tie up with the Carlos DeFalgia thing."

"All right," Barney said. "I'll buy that."

"What about your brother?" Alvarez asked.

"What about him?" Barney stiffened.

"Where's he been all day?"

"He'll tell you when he shows up," Barney said. "Henry's all right. He hasn't anything to do with this."

The sound of the siren wailed to a stop at the front door. Doors banged, feet tramped in the downstairs hall, voices called out. The little cop cursed. "Time's run out, Barney. It's the chief."

"What have you got against him?" Barney asked quickly.

"Nothing much except he's Durand's

210

man and he plays ball with Hurd. He knows the *Lucky Q.* put in at Osterport the day after Carlos was killed, but he's kept it to himself. I've been wondering why. I've also been wondering where Durand was that day," the cop grinned tightly. "I'm not supposed to think on my job, but I can't help it. Good luck to you, Barney. Here comes Petersen. You've got about ten seconds."

Barney looked at the man. Alvarez deliberately turned his back and stood in the bathroom doorway. The full meaning of the cop's behavior burst upon him. And with the realization that he was being offered a chance to escape from the trap, his muscles sprang into action. His fist slashed downward in a sharp, savage blow to the base of Alvarez' neck. The cop staggered forward into the hall, his gun spilling from his pocket. His head struck the opposite wall and he collapsed in a heap, face down on the carpet. Barney leaped over his legs out of the bathroom. A bellow of alarm came from the main stairway and he twisted his head that way, glimpsed the bull head and shoulders of Chief Petersen just reaching the top of the steps. Barney turned and ran for the opposite end of the hall. There was another stairway here, narrow and twisting, once used for servants. It led down to the pantry below. Barney grabbed the newel post and swung around it without slackening speed. Chief Petersen yelled again and there was an echoing shout from below. Barney glimpsed the fat man tugging for his gun and then he tumbled down the narrow staircase, half running and half falling. His legs trembled with the desperate urgency for speed. A shot crashed behind him, shockingly loud inside the house.

He had no thought except to get away from Petersen. Fred Alvarez had given him warning enough what to expect if the chief got his fat hands on him. There would be no mercy, no justice for him in Easterly.

Barney slammed across the dark pantry heading for the kitchen. A cop burst through the opposite doorway at the same moment. It was the big patrolman named Charley. His gun was in his left hand. There was a grin on his hard, angry face. Barney drove a brutal right into the man's belly, crossed with a quick left and the cop fell away from him, arms outflung, crashing into the kitchen table. The gun clattered to the tiled floor. Barney scooped up the .38 on the run, scarcely slackening speed. The back door stuck for a moment when he tugged at it, then it jerked free. Behind him, the house was in an uproar of shouting men and pounding feet. Barney jumped through the kitchen doorway, vaulted the railing of the back porch and hit the turf of the lawn in one smooth rush of movement.

Cold rain slashed at his face. Darkness surrounded him. But he knew every inch of the terrain from childhood and he didn't hesitate. His pounding feet carried him across the lawn toward the low line of shrubbery that marked the property line. A shot crashed behind him, the report flat and vicious in the dark, rainswept night. The bullet spattered on the stone wall behind the line of bare forsythia bushes. He dragged air into his lungs through his burning throat and smashed through the shrubbery in a long flat dive that carried him over the three-foot wall onto the next lawn. Another shot slammed through the night. Barney rolled over, found his feet and ran in a low crouch for the back of the next house.

A confusion of shouts followed him. One of the cops got the prowl car and turned it into the driveway, spotlight blazing over the lawn behind him. Barney forced an extra burst of speed from his trembling muscles and ducked to the right, down the sloping hill. The houses here were spaced far apart on half-acre plots. Lights flashed on in the first one, then another and another. The spotlight swept over the backs of the houses that were on the next street. Barney drew a sobbing breath, felt his feet hit the yielding gravel of a driveway and twisted around the dark bulk of a garage. Pursuit was only thirty yards behind him. Rain poured off the edge of the garage in a steady sheet, drenching him. His lungs felt on fire, but he didn't stop. He pushed away from the garage wall, ran around the house it belonged to and came out on the street below Orient.

Nobody was in sight. Rain beat down

sullenly on the red brick sidewalk, whispering in the barren trees and shrubbery and he turned left, trotting across the dark lawns toward the nearest corner. Headlights warned him before he reached it and he threw himself flat behind the wide trunk of an old chestnut tree, hugging the wet turf. The police car came around the corner fast, skidding through a puddle and sending a sheet of solid water up on the lawns. The siren yowled. The car shot past him, then braked and two prowlies tumbled out, guns in their hands. They ran up the driveway he had just left.

Barney got to his feet in a smooth lunge and turned the corner. His legs trembled. He didn't know how far they would carry him. His head still pulsed with pain and he staggered a little, slipped to one knee, got up and ran on again. At the next corner he was on Orient Street again, two blocks down from his house. There was a tangle of lights and cars back there. He ducked across Orient midway down the next block, then walked between two houses to the back driveway that paralleled the street. It was dark and wet and quiet back here. He began to breathe a little easier. He paused, came to a halt and felt his legs start to go from under him. He couldn't go any further. He wondered if he had made a mistake. Maybe the best thing to do would be to go back there and give himself up. Then he thought of Petersen's exultant face and picked himself up again and started trotting along the sand driveway behind the big houses.

Twice he paused and hid to let searching cops run by. Each time he found himself closer to his house but on the opposite side of the street behind the houses that faced his own. It was his only chance. By doubling back inside the circle of searching men, he might find temporary safety. Then he saw the back of the Durand house, massive in its stone architecture and he knew where his instinct had led him. But it was too soon to try that. He found a niche between the incinerator can and a board fence and sank down on his haunches, sucking air into his aching lungs.

Darkness crept over his mind. The

rain made a hypnotic, metallic tattoo on the rusty incinerator. The darkness warmed and comforted him. It would be easy to give up and let go, to sink into its beckoning black oblivion. He fought his eyes open again with a start. He was shivering, soaked through by the cold, penetrating rain. He felt confused, wondering when this had all started. It seemed an eternity since he had fought Reagan in that hot, garish ring, walled in by the screams of the crowd. Another eternity since he came home and found Lil with the harpoon through her. He remembered his repetitive dream of running down a blind alley only to have a net fall over him and trap him. He was in the net now, caught good and tight. There was no way out. But there had to be a way out. He had been running toward it just now. He couldn't remember his goal. Groaning, he held his aching head, trying to remember.

"Jo," he murmured.

Slowly he climbed to his feet, clinging to the wet, rusted incinerator. Rain slapped coldly at his face, helping to revive him. From far down the sandy driveway came the flicker of flashlights working slowly toward his hiding place. He moved forward as if in a nightmare toward the back of the Durand house. The lawn was dark. More by instinct than rational activity, he found the little side door that led into the shedlike summer kitchen. The door creaked as he closed it softly behind him. He leaned back against it, shutting out the darkness and the incessant beat of the rain and let out his breath in a long, exhaustive sigh.

Something made a steady, irregular crackling sound nearby. He could see nothing in the little shed. He moved forward, straining all his senses, careful not to knock anything over and raise a clatter. His groping fingers found the opposite door that led into the kitchen proper. It had a wrought iron thumb latch and he brought pressure on it carefully, cracked the door an inch and looked through.

There was a triangular brick fireplace built into a corner of the big kitchen and the crackling sound came from the fire that leaped and sang on the hearth. In the warm red light that streamed from it, he saw Jo Durand kneeling on the Belgian tiles of the floor. The firelight tangled with her honey-colored hair and made the pearls she wore gleam with a soft opalescence. She wore a tan cashmere sweater and skirt and knee-length English woolen socks.

Beside her was a small open Gladstone bag and she was carefully spreading a man's fishing gear, pants, boots and windbreaker, to dry before the hot flames. Barney took a chance and opened the door all the way and stepped into the kitchen.

The sound of his movement brought the girl spinning around on her heels, half rising. Her mouth opened as she saw him standing there.

"Please," Barney whispered. "Help me, Jo."

13

THE wind and the rain slashed at the surface of the sea and set up odd, twisting currents that circled down below the storm-lashed ocean into the quiet dark depths, creating a strange unrest in the cold deep. The uneasy pressures rose and fell, winding sinuously through the wreckage of the Orpheus.

The body tugged at its snare with renewed strength. In its stiffness of death it rose a little, caught by a barb that went through one sleeve of its coat. It pulled at the barb as if imbued with a strange, unnatural rebirth of life in its rigid limbs. It lifted again, tugging. The current pushed and helped. A small fragment of the rotting cloth gave way in a jagged, triangular tear. The moldering wreck of the old logging schooner seemed to tremble in the pressure of the tide. A faint grating noise came from its crumbling lower decks. It tilted slightly. The body tugged again at the jagged *piece of iron that held it a prisoner on its deck. The rip lengthened suddenly like the unraveling of knitted wool and the arm came free.*

The body floated up and rolled over and over, moving as if in slow motion. It bumped against the jagged stump of the mizzen mast, came around it and drifted over the fantail of the schooner. There was an eagerness in the way it accepted the help of the tidal current. The rigid blue face seemed to be gleeful in its escape, grinning with lips widespread over the yellowed old teeth as it resumed at last its predestined course toward the distant shore.

★ ★ ★

Jo Durand said: "Did anyone see you come in?"

"I don't think so," said Barney. "No, I'm sure of it."

He watched her as she moistened a cloth under the hot water tap and washed away the dirt and grime and blood from his face. Her eyes were solicitous, anxious, without fear. She looked clean and lovely and wonderful. He didn't have the strength to lift his arms and hold her, however much he wanted to. Then she got some iodine from a cabinet near the kitchen sink and carefully applied it to his cut scalp. The antiseptic stung, helping to revive him. She brought him two aspirins and he swallowed them, drew a deep breath and looked at the dancing flames on the triangular brick hearth. The big kitchen was warm and safe.

"Is Mal at home?" he whispered.

"Chief Petersen came for him," Jo said. "He went out with the police. Nobody else is in the house except us." Then she paused. "Is it true — about that girl?"

"Yes. She's dead."

"Murdered, Petersen said."

"Yes."

Her eyes didn't question him. She accepted his presence almost matter-of-factly, offering him help and temporary safety without saying anything about it. Barney sat on a chair in a corner of the kitchen where he wasn't visible to the cops who went by along the sandy road behind the house. He didn't think they would stop to look for him here of all places. He looked at the clock over the stove and saw that only ten minutes had gone by since he had struck down Fred Alvarez and burst from the house across the street. It seemed more like ten centuries.

"You will help me?" Barney asked.

"Of course," Jo nodded.

"I'll need a place to hide."

"Why did you run?" she asked. "Was it necessary?"

He grinned wryly. "It was either that or let Chief Petersen play tiddly-winks with my ribs and toes."

She shuddered. "He's afraid of you and he hates you because you've persisted in asking questions about the DeFalgia brothers."

"I don't intend to stop now either," Barney said.

"But what can you do?"

"Learn the truth," he said. "And find out why Lil was killed."

"Do you think the two things go together?"

"I'm sure of it," he nodded.

"But I don't see — "

"I don't see myself too clearly. But I've got a few ideas. You've got to trust me, Jo."

"I do," she said quickly. "I do, Barney."

"You didn't go down to Boston to see me fight."

"I didn't want to. I didn't like the idea of your — " she paused and shrugged, "I listened to it on the radio."

"Did Mal?"

She hesitated. "Yes."

"Did you see my brother Henry at any time today?"

She didn't look at him. "Yes."

"Here?"

"He came over to see Mal. They've been bitter enemies, you know. Henry said a great many irresponsible things about Mal. He came over here this morning in his usual temper and quarreled with Mal. I don't know what it was about. I didn't want to listen. And then Henry said he was going to Osterport to prove something."

"Osterport?"

"I couldn't help overhearing it. He was shouting at Mal."

"And he hasn't come back yet?"

"Not that I know of."

"What did Mal do all day?"

"I don't know. He went to the bank, I suppose, and the cannery. We didn't see much of each other. He was home for dinner, that's all, and then he was out all evening and just came back a moment or two before I heard the police sirens." Jo's eyes were wide, staring at him. "Barney, don't think of it."

"Think of what?" he asked.

"Mal."

"Why not?" he asked. "Why not Mal, Jo?"

"I — I feel disloyal," she said.

"But you don't love him."

"No."

"You've been unhappy with him."

"That's beside the point."

"And you love me," Barney said. "Just as I love you, Jo."

She turned away from him quickly and went to the fire and stood with her slim, straight back to him so that he couldn't see her face. The firelight made an aura of her soft, silken hair. He stood up, but he didn't cross the kitchen toward her.

225

It was quiet in the house, quiet outside now. The pursuit had moved outward from the neighborhood like the ripples from a stone thrown into a pond and they were in the undisturbed center of it, safe for the moment. He felt better. He had a purpose, he saw the way ahead with a certain amount of clarity that hadn't been present before. The prospect out there wasn't good. It would taste bitter. But he had to go through with it.

Jo whispered: "Please don't say it like that, Barney."

"I mean it," he said.

"It's too late for us. I made a mistake."

"We both made mistakes," he said. "But they can be corrected."

She turned to face him suddenly. She looked white and strained. Her arms were folded across her firm, round breasts that thrust against the soft fabric of her sweater.

"What do you want me to say?" she asked bitterly. "How do you want me to help you, Barney?"

He said softly: "Tell me about Mal."

"There's nothing to tell."

"Don't be foolish in your loyalty, Jo.

If he's a murderer, I'm going to prove it and you're going to have to face it."

"I don't know," she whispered. "I don't know anything."

"Where was he the day Pedro was killed?"

"In Boston."

"You're sure of that?"

"Reasonably so. I see no reason to doubt it."

"When did he get back to Easterly?"

"On the 6:05 train."

Barney crossed the room toward her and picked up the fishing togs she had taken from the battered Gladstone bag when he first came in. Her eyes followed him, wide and frightened. She started to say something, then was silent as he examined the clothing. None of it looked as if it had been put to hard physical use. The cowhide boots were relatively unscarred. An odor of mildew came from the blue peacoat when he picked it up and then put it aside on the bricks of the hearth.

"Is that Mal's bag?" Barney asked quietly.

Jo nodded mutely.

"The one he took to Boston?"

"Yes."

"But you found this clothing in it?"

"About an hour ago."

Barney drew a deep breath. He did not allow his exultation to show on his dark, battered face.

"Mal didn't go to Boston that day."

"He said he did," Jo whispered.

"You know better."

"I haven't thought about it," she said.

Barney held her shoulders in his hands and forced her to face him. "You mean you haven't wanted to think about it, Jo because of your misguided sense of loyalty to him. You didn't want to face the fact that he lied to you and tried to create an alibi by claiming he was in Boston the day Pedro and Carlos were killed."

"You can't prove otherwise," she whispered.

"I'm going to try."

"Barney, please. he's dangerous — "

"He went to sea," Barney said. "He was on the *Lucky Q*."

"How can you prove it?"

"I'll prove it," he said.

The gun he had taken from the cop named Charley sagged in his pocket. He took it out, snapped open the cylinder and spun it in his fingers. The revolver was fully loaded. Jo watched him with wide, worried eyes. She shivered. Barney thought of Gus Santini. Gus had framed him very well, but he didn't think the fight manager had had any idea of what he was doing. He put Gus out of his mind. His purpose was clear and simple.

"Was Mal with Lil at any time today, Jo?" he asked.

"I don't know. Please put away that gun. What do you think you're going to do with it?"

"Find a murderer," he said.

"It isn't Mal," she said.

"Why are you so sure?"

"I don't know. But I *am* sure, Barney." Her voice pleaded with him. "Mal may have a lot of faults, but I don't think he would kill anyone. He — "

The front door slammed.

Jo looked stricken. Her mouth opened, then she made a quick gesture toward Barney and left the kitchen for the front hall. A man's voice said something, the words quick and angry. Barney faded back toward the shed behind the kitchen. He kept the gun in his hand. Then Jo's footsteps returned.

"Barney?"

He stepped out of the shadows of the shed doorway. The man with her was his brother Henry. Henry's eyes flicked from Barney's face to the gun and then back again. He looked drawn and haggard and a muscle twitched in a tic under his right eye. He wore no hat or coat and his clothing was sopping wet. Water dripped from his hands to the polished red tiles of the kitchen floor. His blonde hair was flattened to his long, patrician head.

"What are you doing with that gun, Barnabas?" he asked.

Barney countered with his own question. "Are you alone?"

"Of course. I've just come from the house. The chief tells me you killed that trollop you brought into my house."

"Do you believe that?" Barney asked.

"I don't know what to believe. I don't understand it. I'm waiting for an explanation from you as to why you ran away from the police before they could question you. I understand you quarreled with the girl and that she stole some more money from you. Is that true?"

"Not all of it," Barney said. "There was no quarrel and I didn't kill her, Henry."

His brother looked doubtful. He fixed Jo with dour eyes. "Where is Mal?"

"With the police, I think."

"I went to Osterport," Henry offered suddenly. "I was looking for him there. But I didn't learn anything. I'm sure he was there last week when Pedro was killed, but nobody would talk to me." He seemed to be speaking to himself, his eyes fixed on the flames that crackled in the kitchen fireplace. His hands shook, and the tic under his eye became more pronounced. "I don't know what to say. I don't know what to think. What has happened doesn't seem rational."

"Who did you talk to in Osterport?" Barney asked.

Henry looked at him startled. "A man named Bryson Jay. He runs a ship's chandlery up there. But he wouldn't talk to me. He threw me out. He said

I was crazy to talk that way about Mal Durand."

"Is Bryson Jay connected with Peter Hurd?" Barney asked.

"He does some outfitting of his fishing boats."

"I'd better go up there," Barney said. "I'll make him talk."

Jo touched him quickly. "You can't take such a chance, Barney. The police are looking for you now and you'd be caught before you got a mile from this house."

"There's nothing else I can do," Barney said. "I can't stay here."

"Come back to our house," Henry said. "You can hide there."

Barney shook his head, stifling his impatience. "Neither of you seems to understand. Hiding won't do any good. I can't hide forever. The only chance I've got to dig my way out of this mess is to learn the truth and I'll never get anywhere if I crawl into some dark hole and stay there. I've got a lot of questions to ask and I'm going to get the answers."

"How will you get to Osterport?" Jo

asked. "It's almost thirty miles up the coast."

Barney grinned and kissed her. "I'll use your car. If the police or Durand ask any embarrassing questions, just tell them I stole it."

Jo nodded. "I'll get the keys."

14

EASTERLY Depot was dark except for the light in the stationmaster's window. It was a long, ramshackle, shed-type building, gray and weathered, with the roof of the train platform curled and warped by sixty years of New England weather. The midnight train from Boston had pulled out ten minutes before and the dozen or so passengers had dissipated into the surrounding streets, on foot and by taxi. Barney remained in the big Cadillac parked across the square from the depot, hidden in the darkness. He'd had no trouble leaving Orient Street in Jo's car. He saw no police at the depot. Inside closing up for the day, was Kelcey Green, the stationmaster. When no one had stirred or moved near the depot for five more minutes, Barney got out of the car and crossed the square to the station building.

Kelcey Green was an old man who had been ancient when Barney was a boy playing around the railroad tracks. He wore bifocals, had a thick mop of unruly white hair and a dour manner. He peered over the glasses as Barney entered the hot little office and grunted.

"The conquering hero," he said. "Little Barney Hammond. Heard your fight, son. Thought you were going to get licked. Glad you didn't lose though. Had fifty cents bet on you. Damn fool to bet."

"Thanks," Barney said interrupting the staccato flow. Old man Kelcey was the opposite of the taciturn Yankee. Once he started talking he jumped from one subject to another in an interminable stream of brittle words. "Have you seen Chief Petersen, Kelcey?"

The old man peered over his glasses again. "Here about half an hour ago. Told me to let him know if you took the 12:05 out of town. Guess you missed it, son."

"I wasn't trying to make it. I just wanted to ask you about Mal Durand's trip to Boston last week."

The old man snickered. "You and Chief Petersen, hey?"

"Did he ask you about it, too?"

"Sure did. Told him I couldn't remember a thing about it. Got to tell you the same thing, too."

"Durand didn't make the trip?"

"Couldn't say. Can't keep tabs on everybody. Just didn't happen to see him. That don't mean he didn't get on or off the train when I wasn't looking. Can't help you, son."

"All right," Barney said. "What about Samson, the taxi-driver?"

"Same thing. Petersen collared him and yelled a lot of questions that just scared Samson speechless." Kelcey Green chuckled. "Fat slob. Poor old Sam couldn't say a word."

"He didn't see Durand either?"

"Nope."

"All right," Barney said. "Thanks a lot."

Barney grinned and flipped a hand at the old man and went back to the Cadillac. He was feeling better. His head felt clear, his mind was geared to the single purpose of his thoughts. A pattern had formed that fitted everything that had happened and his spirits lifted with the hope that there was a grim answer to

236

the murders that had plagued the town. The answer existed and all that remained was to dig it out.

Tal Carter's office at the Town Landing was dark and Barney headed for the inn where the pier superintendent lived in a bachelor room. The inn was no competition for Easterly House; it was a residential hotel and boarding house for waterfront workers and single fishermen. Barney went in the back way, up a flight of old iron fire-escape stairs to the third floor and down the hall to Tal's room. There was the stale odor of fried food, the muted music from a radio, the clink of a glass from other doors he passed. A thin slab of yellow light came from under Carter's door. Barney paused to listen, but there was no sound from inside. He waited another moment, looking up and down the drab hotel hallway and then knocked. A bedspring creaked and Carter's voice came muttering through the door panel. Barney knocked again, more insistently.

Carter opened the door, wrapping a faded gray bathrobe around his flabby body. His bald head gleamed in the light behind him. He regarded Barney with a mixture of surprise and fear.

"Man, are you crazy? Don't you know the cops are looking for you? Get in here, quick."

Nobody else was in the dingy little room. The bed was mussed and a weekly magazine lay on the floor beside it where it had slipped when Tal got out of bed. A can of beer and a bowl of apples stood on the table nearby and reminded Barney that he'd had practically nothing to eat all day. He bit into one of the apples while Tal closed the door and turned back to him.

"What happened?" Carter asked. "I heard your girl was killed — "

"She wasn't my girl," Barney said.

"But Petersen said — "

"To hell with Petersen," Barney snapped. "And I didn't kill her, Tal."

"Well, if you say so, I believe you, Barney. But you're really in bad trouble this time. Why did you come here?"

"For help," Barney said.

"Well, of course, I'll do anything I can — "

Barney saw the fear in the chubby

man's eyes, the obvious reluctance in his voice that belied his quick words. It didn't matter. He didn't blame Tal for feeling the way he did. He told Carter the ideas that had come to him since he'd found Lil murdered and Tal kept shaking his head negatively. A light beading of sweat stood out on the man's round face. Once Carter went to the door and looked up and down the hallway while Barney talked. He locked the door afterward and Barney didn't miss his trembling fingers. He finished another apple before he stopped talking.

"No," Carter said. "I don't believe it, Barney."

"It's got to be that way. It fits," Barney insisted. "All I've got to prove is that Durand was in Osterport instead of Boston."

"I still don't see why you pick Mal. It could have been anybody. He could have hired any one of a dozen men to do the job."

"I've got that figured out, too," Barney said.

"But Durand!" Carter looked even more frightened than before. "I don't want any part of it, Barney. You don't know how it's been with me. I've had a tough time. If I lose my job at the Fish Pier, I don't know what I'll do. I can't take a chance with it."

"Just tell me about the *Lucky Q.*," Barney said.

"I can't, Barney. Don't ask me about it."

Barney stood up. His voice was flat. "Are you taking Durand's money, Tal?"

"He gives me a little bonus every now and then — "

"So that makes you his pet slave?"

"It doesn't make me anything!" Carter's voice was louder. I just don't think you're right about any of this. According to what you told me, I don't think this girl's death has anything to do with Mal Durand. You ought to be checking on that fight manager of yours instead of poking around back here and stirring up more trouble. If you had any sense, you wouldn't have run away from the cops. If you're innocent, you've got nothing to be afraid of. All they can do is hold you for a little while for questioning. Look, Barney, if you turn yourself in, I'll take care of getting a lawyer and everything, I'll do everything I can — "

"Never mind. I'm sorry, Tal."

"I'd like to help you, but — "

"It's all right. I won't get you into any trouble, Tal. I'll get out right now. Just answer one question for me. Tell me about this fellow, Bryson Jay."

"Jay? He's up in Osterport."

"Who is he? Where can I find him?"

"He's got a job like mine up there. Runs a chandlery and a fish pier. He lives up on King's Road. What's he got to do with it?"

"Maybe nothing," Barney said. He paused with his hand on the door. "You won't call the cops about my being here, will you, Tal?"

"Of course not, Barney!"

The man's voice was too loud, too hearty in its assurance to ring true. Barney felt a twist of pity for the timid man. He picked another apple from the bowl, said "Thanks," and looked up and down the dim hotel corridor. Nobody was in sight. He let himself out, moved quickly to the back of the inn and clattered down the fire-escape to the alley where he had left Jo's car. The rain had slackened to a steady drizzle. Barney looked up at Tal's window and saw the man draw the window shade and then his shadow crossed it and moved away. He could imagine Tal at the telephone dialing either the police or Mal Durand. It was time to get away from there.

Osterport was a little village of only two or three hundred families built around a rocky little cove that was used by fishing boats as an emergency shelter from winter storms. Its fishing fleet consisted of only a half dozen boats. In the summer it was an off-trail tourist spot and boasted of a barn theatre and an art colony. Barney turned off the main highway and saw the few dim street lights twinkling in the dark rain. It was two o'clock in the morning and the tires of Jo's heavy car made a lonely whining sound on the wet asphalt as he turned toward the waterfront. There had been no other traffic on the twisting coastal road he had chosen to follow. He parked the Cadillac in the shadows of a high board fence and got out on the wet sidewalk, scanning the dark waterfront street. The smell of muddy tidal flats was strong and pungent in the night air and a fog had begun to mingle with the light rain.

The sign over the big barnlike building had Bryson Jay's name on it. Barney leaned against the board fence and watched it for five minutes. No lights shone anywhere up and down the street. Nobody moved along the sidewalk. A bar down at the corner was closed and dark except for a sputtering green neon sign in the grimy window. He waited another five minutes then went back to the car and took a flashlight from the glove compartment. The familiar scent of Jo's perfume came from the little cubby-hole. He shut the car door so it wouldn't slam and crossed the wet street to try the door to the sail loft. It was locked tight. Two big overhead doors next to it were padlocked and chained. A narrow alley nearby brought him to the back of the building. There was a loading platform along the back of the loft and more overhead doors, all of them equally secured. Barney jumped up on the platform, feeling his way through the darkness and found a back door to the office that was fastened by a simple ward lock. He went back along the platform using the flashlight intermittently and found an iron bar that looked small enough, then returned and forced the simple lock with a quick snap of the bar. The crack of splintering wood seemed abnormally loud against the overtones of the rain.

Darkness yawned beyond the doorway. Barney checked the loading platform and the street once more then stepped quietly inside and pushed the door shut as far as it would go. The broken lock prevented it from closing completely. He waited, smelling the familiar odors of canvas and netting and old seasoned lumber. The darkness was absolute. After a minute or two he tried the flashlight and found himself in a wide hallway that ran toward the front of the building facing the wharves. A flight of stairs led upward to the office. He went up carrying the iron bar and flashlight with him. Something scurried down the hallway below him and he decided it was a rat. It didn't bother him. An office door with Bryson Jay's name on it again barred his way.

This one wasn't locked and he let himself inside with a quick sigh of relief.

The place was very similar to Tal Carter's back in Easterly. There were ships' clearances in a neat pile on the work worn desk and a series of low filing cabinets on either side of the window. Barney started on the desk papers, assuming they would be the most recent reports of arrivals and departures. They were. But there was nothing that mentioned the Easterly dragger, *Lucky Q*.

He went through the sheaf of papers twice then tried the desk drawers. They were locked by means of a catch in the center drawer and a few moments' of careful work released them all. He began going through them quickly, his senses alert for any warning sound from below. The rain stopped outside, replaced by a white fog that pressed cottony hands against the black window. There was a gun in the desk, a big Colt .45, and he examined it briefly, checking the fully loaded magazine and sniffing the barrel and then put it back on the oil-stained paper it had been resting on. There was a half empty bottle of rum in one of the larger bottom drawers. Several old and dirtied handkerchiefs and a bottle of ephedrine nose drops. A tangle of papers that needed sorting, bills and invoices, a fresh checkbook indicating a balance of eleven hundred and twenty-two dollars and nothing else. Nothing with the name *Lucky Q.* on it.

Barney straightened, aware of disappointment, aware of the pressure of time that gave him only so much grace in here before it became dangerous. The filing cabinets that flanked the window were secured with a much more formidable lock than the desk. He hated to tackle it. The cabinets would be impossible to open without leaving a certain sign of his intrusion. Then he decided it didn't matter and started toward them with the wrecking bar.

A door slammed like a pistol shot downstairs.

Instantly Barney thumbed the flashlight, returning the office to darkness. Footsteps sounded in the lower hallway. There was more than just one pair of them. Two men had come in and now he heard their voices, one high and querulous and protesting, the other heavy and angry. They started heavily up the stairs.

Swinging around the desk, Barney crossed the dark office in a long stride, heading for a closet door in the opposite wall. It wasn't locked. He stepped inside quickly, felt the smothering wet-wool closeness of old clothing and pulled the door to until it was almost closed. The office light flashed on only a moment later. The front door was opened and the two men came in. Barney crouched in his hiding place, with only a small sliver of the office visible to him from the narrow closet. The two men crossed briefly in front of his vision and he saw the first was a spare, middle-aged man with lank gray hair and a long, worried face with small, frightened, resentful eyes. He was being pushed forward against his high-pitched protests by Peter Hurd.

The Easterly waterfront boss looked big and bulky in his gray overcoat, his broad, blocky face half shadowed under the brim of his hat. Barney guessed that the first man was Bryson Jay. Hurd shoved the man stumbling past his desk, then grabbed the other's coat lapels and slammed him down into the chair behind it with enough strength to make Jay bounce. A squeal of protest came from the chandler and dock master.

"Now, wait a minute, Mr. Hurd, you can't do this — "

"I'm doing it," Hurd said heavily. "Have you seen him at all tonight?"

"No. Nobody. His brother was here earlier today and I had some of the boys get rid of him. I didn't talk to Hammond at all!" Bryson Jay's words seemed to tumble all over themselves in his anxiety to get them out. A dribble of saliva ran down his long, unshaven jaw. He looked as if he had been yanked out of bed by physical force and had his clothing thrown at him. His stringy knitted tie was halfway around his collar, almost under his ear. His hands shook as he held them up to ward off Hurd. "I'm telling you the truth, Mr. Hurd. You know I don't mind cooperating in anything you say. It's nothing to me, one way or the other, you understand. I don't know why it's so important, but if you say it is, that's all right with me."

Hurd looked dissatisfied. His hooded eyes gleamed thoughtfully as he stood over the frightened man and he rubbed one hand along the hard ridge of his jaw in speculation. Barney scarcely breathed in the stuffy narrow closet. His legs trembled from being forced to maintain his crouch. Hurd moved toward the window, out of his line of vision. The man at the desk followed him with quick, sly eyes. Hurd's voice came back at him like a whip, demanding to know if he had done anything with the papers. The man at the desk shook his head.

"I have them in the filing cabinet."

"Give them to me," Hurd demanded.

"But I can't do that. It's part of the port records — "

"You don't understand," Hurd said quietly. "The *Lucky Q.* never came in here that day. And if she didn't come in, then there can't be any official records of her arrival or departure, can there? That wouldn't be logical, Mr. Jay."

"I can't — "

"Open that cabinet and give me the paper," Hurd snapped.

The man at the desk sighed and stood

up and moved out of Barney's sight. There came the sound of a key in the cabinet lock and then the rolling of drawers being pulled out and the shuffling crackle of papers. Hurd's voice was impatient, demanding that the man hurry.

"I shouldn't do this, Mr. Hurd. It's not right — "

A sharp slap cracked in the office and there came the thump of Bryson Jay's shoulder hitting the wall. Barney shifted his position slightly. Jay started to wail in protest and Hurd hit him again.

"Here it is," Jay said quickly. "Right here. Take it."

"That's better." Hurd's voice was thick with satisfaction. "And remember what I said before. You don't mention this to anybody."

"But suppose the police ask me about this paper? Suppose they want to know if the *Lucky Q.* was here that day?"

"You tell them what I said. She didn't put in. Nobody saw her. Nobody will mention it. You don't have anything to worry about, Mr. Jay. Nothing, that is, except me."

"Yes, sir, Mr. Hurd."

"Remember that."

"Yes, sir, but — "

"But what?" Hurd snapped.

"Other people *did* see the *Lucky Q*. What will you do about them?"

There came the sound of another blow, the crash of a body striking the wall. Barney felt the impact through the closet door.

"You forget too quickly," Hurd grated. "I told you not to worry about anything but what I said. Now pick yourself up and let's get out of here."

The two men moved across Barney's range of vision, Bryson Jay holding his hand over his mouth with blood trickling through his shaking fingers. The light went out. The door was closed. Barney waited for a count of ten, then straightened from his awkward position and quit the closet to move across the darkened office. The downstairs door slammed. Quickly he followed down the stairs to the lower hall and ducked out through the back entrance by which he had entered. The fog was thick, smelling of the sea as it curled down the alley to the loading platform. At the mouth of the alley he paused, straining to see through the white gloom. From somewhere nearby a car motor started up, then headlights made a bright glare through the slow moving mists. He stepped back a little until the car passed then broke into a run for the Cadillac parked half a block up the street. He was less than a minute behind Peter Hurd when he reached the highway that curved south along the coast back toward Easterly.

15

THE fog was thicker when, a few minutes before three in the morning, Barney turned Jo's car into Water Street, driving without lights. Peter Hurd had driven like a maniac along the treacherous road back to town and Barney had followed, just keeping the other car's red tail-lights in sight. Beyond the Town Landing, Water Street curved into an area of shabby fishermen's shacks, old wharf buildings and tumbled down sheds opposite Five Penny Island and Barney dropped a little farther behind, easing the big car over the ruts and bumps in the old cobblestone street. Hurd turned right into the heart of the slum district then left again and stopped beyond the next corner in front of a small, gray, shingled house that sat back from the street behind a sagging and broken picket fence.

The house was in darkness except for a dim glow from a back window. Barney stopped his car a block away, leaving it in deep shadow and walked up the alley to the back of the house. Hurd was already inside when he reached a point where he could look into the window. Fog had misted the dirty gray panes making the interior vague and uncertain. Barney slipped inside the picket fence and came up close to the wall of the house, picking his way over the unseen tin cans and junk that littered the narrow yard. The shade was partly drawn, but he could see inside fairly well from this position.

The room seemed to be a bedroom that was also used as a study or workshop of some kind. For a moment Barney didn't recognize the electrical equipment that filled the long table against the opposite wall, the components being arranged in helter-skelter fashion. Then he suddenly let his breath out in a long sigh and stepped back a little to study the roof of the shabby cottage. A new and shining transmitting aerial gleamed through the twisting tendrils of fog. It was an amateur radio outfit.

The man who lived in the house had his back to the window, facing Hurd's bulky, menacing figure. Their voices did not carry outside except in a subdued, sullen monotone. The man's back and slight figure seemed faintly familiar to Barney. He wore a blue robe and cotton pajamas and his feet were stuck into scuffed leather slippers. His hair was sandy and awry and while he talked he took quick gulps from the liquor glass that stood among the tangled radio equipment on the table.

Then the man turned and Barney saw it was Carl Macklin, the assistant engineer who had sailed on the last cruise of the *Mary Hammond*.

The traitor, Barney thought.

The man was expostulating with Hurd, denying something to judge from his gestures and the vehemence on his round face and sharp-nosed features. His straight hair hung in loops over his sweaty forehead. He wasn't afraid; he seemed to be drunk, from the way he moved about the room. Barney felt impatient to hear what was being said, but there seemed to be no way to accomplish that unless he entered the house, too. And that was impossible without detection.

Hurd's visit to Macklin was brief. His voice rumbled in a menacing murmur and he picked up a liquor bottle and broke it on the floor, apparently as a warning to Macklin not to drink. Then he quit the room and Barney moved away from the window to watch the waterfront boss return to his car. Barney hesitated, wondering whether to continue to trail the man. Carl Macklin seemed to be a more interesting prospect. He remembered how Pedro DeFalgia had come to him aboard the *Mary Hammond* and insisted that a traitor among the schooner's crew had used the radio to contact Hurd and give away the schooner's position. And Pedro had been right. Barney's anger grew as he waited until Hurd's car was out of sight, then crossed the barren front yard and tried the door. Macklin had locked it. Barney knocked impatiently and waited until something moved behind the dingy curtains. The door opened about two inches.

"Mr. Hurd, I thought you said — "

Barney drove a shoulder against the door, slamming it inward and driving the man backward down the little hallway. Macklin yelped in surprise and alarm, scrambled to his feet and started to retreat down the hallway. Barney kicked the door shut and dove for him, caught him by one arm and spun him around. Macklin crashed into the wall with a thump that shook the little house.

"Hold it," Barney growled.

The man struggled in his grip. "Let go of me!"

He tried to break away. His bathrobe tore in Barney's hands and he went staggering down the narrow hallway. The odor of liquor was strong and rank on Macklin's breath. Barney took a long stride and caught him in the doorway to the room he had been watching.

"You're going to talk to me, Carl," Barney said.

"I haven't done anything! You've got no right — "

"What was Hurd doing here?"

"Hurd?"

"I saw him come in and talk to you. What did he want?"

"Nothing! I swear it!"

"You're lying," Barney said. "You're

the one who swiped the radio key on the *Mary Hammond* and got a message to Hurd telling him where we were fishing!"

"No!"

Barney hit him. All his pent-up frustration and anger went into the blow. His fist cracked sharply on the man's jaw and Macklin toppled backward, crashed into a swivel chair by the radio table and splintered it. Blood trickled from his mouth. His eyes were wild. He started to get up and Barney bent over him and grabbed the loose lapels of the robe and yanked him savagely to his feet.

"You're the one who sold out Cap'n Henry," Barney grated.

"No!"

"How much is Hurd paying you to spy for him?"

"Nothing!"

Barney hit him again. Macklin crashed into the table and sent the component parts of his ham radio outfit skittering in all directions as his arms flailed for a grip. One of the units crashed to the floor in a shower of broken tubes and twisted, torn wires. Macklin wailed and stooped to pick it up. Barney kicked it aside and Macklin straightened, shrinking away from him toward the bed.

"You've got no right to do this," the man whispered. "The cops are looking for you. They say you killed that blonde girl of yours. They'll get you, Barney Hammond. I'll tell 'em you were here, too."

"Not until you tell me what I want to know."

"There's nothing to tell!" Macklin protested.

"What was Hurd doing here?"

"He — he wanted to know if I'd work for him."

"How? In what kind of a job?"

"On one of his fishing boats, that's all. He's trying to buy up your brother Henry's crew so he won't have any men to take the schooner out when he's ready to fish again!" Macklin's voice grew stronger and more certain. "That's what he came for. I swear it."

"You're lying," Barney said. "You're already in Hurd's pay."

"No!"

"He came here to remind you to

keep your mouth shut about the way you contacted the *Lucky Q*. Isn't that right?"

"No!"

Barney said quietly: "I've got all night, Carl. It's a pleasure to work over a rat like you. I'll enjoy doing it."

The man's eyes rolled in fright. He squeezed himself farther back into a corner of the room by the bed. Blood ran in a bright red wriggle down his chin and stained his robe. He swiped at it with a trembling hand.

"Please, Barney. Don't."

"Then tell me the truth."

"I can't. I'm afraid."

"Of Hurd?"

"He'll kill me!"

"Has he killed anyone else? Did he kill Pedro and Carlos?"

"I don't know."

"Or the girl?"

"I don't know."

"But you work for him."

"I — " Macklin started to shake his head then gave a shuddering sigh and nodded very slowly. "I need a drink."

"Later."

"Have a heart, Barney!"

"Later."

Macklin gave up. He sat down slowly on the bed, nursing his battered face. His attitude was one of despair and hopelessness, of a man who had resigned himself to the worst. Barney leaned back against the littered and broken radio table and waited. The house was quiet. He could see the white fog beyond the single drab window in the dingy little room. He could almost smell it.

"You work for Hurd," he said quietly.

"Yes."

"You radioed our position to him last week so he could tear up the *Mary Hammond*'s drag equipment."

"I — I sent him the message. Yes."

"How much did he pay you?"

"Two hundred dollars."

"So you sold us all out for that?"

"I — I needed the money. None of the crew have been paid off yet, Barney. Henry is broke. He's in debt over his head. He'll never get out from under and Hurd has him backed into a corner. He's licked, even if he don't know it yet."

"So you sold out to the winning side,"

Barney said flatly.

"I couldn't help it. He threatened me. He knew I was a radio ham and he figured nobody would suspect if he used my equipment."

"Who did you talk to that day? You spoke over the radio-telephone to the *Lucky Q.* didn't you?"

Macklin nodded. "Yes."

"Who answered your call?"

The man licked his lips. "I don't remember. I don't know."

"You must have recognized the other man's voice!"

"No."

He was lying. It was evident in the abrupt shift of his voice, in the desperation that crept into his frightened eyes. He couldn't meet Barney's gaze. Barney let the silence in the room spin itself out. Sweat glistened on Macklin's face. A clock ticked somewhere, abnormally loud. Barney dipped a hand in his pocket and took out a cigarette and lit it. The gesture startled the other man and he shrank back still farther in his corner by the bed. His bruised mouth hung open. Barney dragged the smoke into his lungs and waited a little longer. Macklin's breathing grew loud in the room.

"That's the truth," Macklin whispered. "What are you waiting for? I've told you what I did. I'm ashamed of it, I'm sorry about it, but I couldn't help it. I didn't want Hurd's gang to go to work on me. I needed money. So I said I would work for him and I did. But that's all I can tell you. That's all I know."

"Not quite," Barney said.

"I tell you I don't know who talked to me on the radio-telephone! I swear it!"

"You know," Barney said. "You'll tell me."

The man's fear was now much worse than it was before. He opened and closed his wide mouth like a fish out of water.

"I can't," Macklin whispered.

"You're afraid?"

"Yes. I'm afraid."

"Worse than you're afraid of what I'll do to you if you don't talk?"

"Yes."

"That isn't reasonable," Barney said. "I've got all night. The cops won't come looking for me here. I can take my time with you, Carl. You'll only be fit for the hospital by morning. Nothing is going to stop me from getting at the truth."

"Ask me anything else," Macklin said. "Anything at all."

Barney said: "You saw Pedro DeFalgia get shot?"

"I saw him fall out of the dory, yes."

"Did you see the *Lucky Q.*?"

"Sure."

"Did you see who shot Pedro from her deck?"

"I didn't see anything like that. I didn't hear any shot. Cap'n Henry told Newfie Joe to keep the fog horn going and it was blasting in my ears all the time the dragger was off our stern. I didn't hear anything at all. All I saw was Pedro falling out of the dory."

Barney said: "All right. Now answer my other question."

"About who I talked to?"

Macklin lunged up without warning and plunged toward the door. His move was quick and took Barney by surprise and he was almost into the hallway when Barney caught him with a leap that brought them both crashing to the floor. Macklin fought with a frenzy inspired by terror, kicking and gouging and trying to get a thumb into Barney's eyes. Barney slapped his clawing hand down, grabbed him by the hair and slammed his head against the floor. Macklin screamed, the sound splitting the early-hour quiet. Barney hit him again, wriggled aside as Macklin tried to knee him in the groin and Macklin screamed again, trying to wake the neighborhood. Barney's gun fell from his pocket with a thump. Macklin grabbed for it, missed and Barney scooped it up, reversed it and slammed the barrel across the man's head as Macklin opened his mouth to yell again. His shout died strangling in his throat. His body went limp under Barney's grip. He was out cold.

Barney let out a long breath of frustration and straightened up, his eyes circling the room. From the house next door came a man's deep shout and a woman's shrill reply. Barney flicked out the light in the room and stepped out into the narrow, dingy hallway and opened the front door of the house. A light came on in the house across the street. Another shone in a cottage two doors down. The whole neighborhood was coming alive, alerted by Macklin's desperate screams.

The gate in the sagging picket fence squealed as he let himself out to the sidewalk. Two men were running toward him from the direction of Jo's parked car. He was cut off from going in that direction. The men saw him and one of them yelled a command to halt. Barney turned to the left and sprinted down the crooked, twisting street.

The fog swallowed him a moment later.

16

THE *Lucky Q.* loomed like a ghost in the thick fog as Barney walked toward her mooring. He had walked back along the waterfront after shaking off the neighbor's pursuit, his stride long and quick with the urgency of desperation. In three more hours it would be dawn and he couldn't hope to evade Chief Petersen's men forever. He was leaving a wide trail behind him that not even the fat cop could miss, so they knew he was still in town. Once Petersen got his big hands on him, he could abandon all hope of getting the positive answers he needed. He had to work quickly and surely to clinch what he had gotten so far.

The wharf was dark and quiet. Nobody challenged him when he scaled the fence that barred the way to the dragger from the street. Apparently there was no watchman on the pier, at least nobody that he could see, although he waited for some ten precious minutes, looking and listening in the shadows of the fog-swathed sheds before he dropped lightly to the fishing boat's deck.

The vessel had been washed down and thoroughly scoured since his visit last week. He felt a little puzzled as to why the *Lucky Q.* hadn't gone out again on another fishing cruise but then dismissed it from his mind and worked his way quietly aft toward the pilot house. The door was unlocked. He still had the flashlight he had taken from Jo's car and he flicked it on carefully, examining the chart table, the radio-direction finder, the radio-telephone. The vessel lifted and fell in the easy swell of the tide and her mooring lines creaked. There was no other sound. There was a strong wooden locker built into one side of the little cabin, about two feet high and Barney worked at the lock for a moment then turned his attention to the gun locker on the opposite wall. There was a padlocked hasp on the door to this cabinet, but it offered little difficulty when he hammered it loose with the gun butt. The hasp snapped and fell to the deck with a metallic clatter and he paused, dousing the light, to listen for any sound of alarm. There was none. There were several weapons on the built-in rack inside the cabinet and he let his light play over them briefly as he dismissed the two 12-gauge shotguns and lifted out the .30-30 rifle and carried it to the chart table for a closer examination. The fog pressed with white hands against the pilot house windows. The dragger stirred uneasily under the lift and fall of the tide. Something creaked and snapped and he lifted his head to listen again. The sound was not repeated.

The rifle in his hands was freshly cleaned and oiled. The magazine clip was full. *They've had a week to cover up*, Barney thought. Without Pedro's body, it would be impossible to connect this gun with the murderous slug that had toppled the old man from the dory. Possibly he could run a bluff with it, but he had little hope of success in that direction. He put the gun back on the rack and closed the locker as best he could then quit the pilot house and walked forward around the ice hatch and fish pens toward the crew's quarters in the fo'castle.

There didn't seem to be any chance of stumbling into anything decisive, but he felt restless and uneasy about quitting the dragger, as if something here had escaped his attention, something he ought to know about. He scanned the wharf once more, saw no sign of anyone and went below.

Down here he used his flashlight to check every bunk. Most of the crew's lockers were securely padlocked and he didn't touch them. Those that were open warranted a quick examination. He found nothing of interest. He was halfway back to the ladder that led up to the deck when he heard footfalls up above.

Instantly he put out the light and paused, scarcely breathing. The footsteps crossed the deck toward the forward compartment where he was hidden. Barney backed up, found another door toward the rear and worked his way into a narrow passage that led to the engine room. Another hatch opened on the deck from here. He waited, pressing his hands against the weight overhead, listening in the darkness for a sound from the other man. All he heard was the quick pumping of his heart. He heard nothing more. Carefully he eased the hatch upward then slid it aside enough to permit him to slip through the narrow gap to the deck.

He never saw the man who waited for him except as a quick blur of movement, a smear of white as the man's hand descended. Darkness crashed through his brain and he fell face down on the dragger's deck. He heard a throaty laugh that went echoing away down the corridors of his mind and then he heard and felt and saw nothing at all.

★ ★ ★

Now the body was free at last, swimming with the strong push of the tide that urged it toward the shore. There was only a short distance to go. Already the strong drive of the surf that roiled up over the shallows, the rocky bottom, was having an effect, turning the body this way and that, rolling it over and over with each successive sea that lifted and raced toward the black shingle.

A long, dark finger of rock thrust out

into the turmoil of the surf, shunting the current southward in a quick missrace of seething foam that ran deep and wide, scouring a channel for itself. The body tumbled and fell into the riptide and went head over heels along with it, bowing to the scudding surface now and then, rolling over and over with the impersonal push and surge of the sea. The point of rock was safely bypassed.

Now the current slowed to a more stately cadence, circling around and around within the confines of a little rocky cove that went by the name of Half-Moon Hollow. There was a small beach of coarse sand at the south shore of the cove, a place for quahogs and crabs to root in and wait for the next tide to wash them to sea again. The beach was littered with all manner of debris, the flotsam and jetsam that the restless ocean spurned. A dory lay on the beach, pulled up out of reach of the tide, bottom up to the foggy sky. Beyond the dory, a small path led up among the rocks, twisting and turning to a rickety wooden landing beyond which was the house of an old oysterman named Ferris

McHugh. Ferris slept soundly, lulled by the ceaseless rush and beat of the surf nearby beyond the Hollow.

Once, twice, and three times the body made a slow circuit of the little cove, riding the slack of the current. The tide was due to change in half an hour. Then the current would ebb, falter and reverse itself as the water was sucked out of the Hollow in a swiftly growing current, to dissipate itself in the deeper channels of Easterly Harbor. Through the dark-white night came the mournful regular tolling of the fog bell at the end of the distant stone breakwater. The sound of it lulled Ferris McHugh deeper into his sleep.

One shoulder of the dead man grazed bottom and his progress faltered. He slid away from the shore and his face for a moment broke through the surface, terrible in its death's grimace, old teeth grinning at the dark and rocky beach. Behind the body, a sea grew and swelled and moved in minor majesty toward the shore. Twenty feet from the dead man, the rest curled over, crashed in a smother of white foam and broke for the shore. The tumble of water snatched up the

dead man and hurtled him to the sand,
forced him higher and higher in the
shallows then ebbed, receding. A second
wave washed over him, stirring his stiff
limbs but did not succeed in dislodging
him. A third and a fourth followed. He
was fast in the grip of the land again.

The tide changed.

Up in the cottage above the Hollow, an
old alarm clock suddenly clattered to life
and rang shrilly. Ferris McHugh groaned
in his sleep, sat up and shut it off.

★ ★ ★

Barney was drowning in torrents of water,
harsh and salty, that sloshed over him,
spattering on his face, smarting his eyes,
trickling down his nose and throat. From
the deep, deep darkness where he had
been, he fought his way up through
interminable heights, struggling against
the water. He gasped and choked and
dragged air deep into his lungs and above
the queer pounding in his head he heard
a voice, deep and thick with satisfaction:
"He's coming around now."

"Give him another bucket."

"You want to drown him?"

"I want to talk to him. Bring him to."

Barney twisted his head violently aside as another torrent of water was poured over him. The movement brought sudden nausea to him and for several minutes afterward he lay in misery, concerned only with the torment of his stomach. A chill gripped him and he shivered and shuddered, huddling in a tight ball on the hard deck where he lay. Light glimmered beyond his tightly shut eyelids. A booted foot prodded him and from a great distance overhead a voice spoke to him impatiently.

"All right," said the second voice. "Leave him alone for a moment."

"I ought to kick his face in."

"You'll get a chance at that later."

Barney opened his eyes. His head throbbed with a steady, repetitive pulse of pain. He rubbed his face and felt the hard clot of dried blood on his neck where it had run down from his broken scalp. He could see nothing except an expanding and contracting aura of dazzling light that glared down on him like a cyclopean eye from far above. Shadows moved beyond the periphery of the circle of light. A face with a head and shoulders bent over him.

"Can you hear me, Hammond?"

Barney worked his stiff mouth. "I hear you."

"Sit up, then."

He tried to sit up. He couldn't make it. He tried again, unwilling that anyone should put his hand on him. The light overhead suddenly contracted into the firm outline of a ship's lantern. He saw he was in the fo'castle of the *Lucky Q.* and he wondered briefly how long he had been out and why he had been dragged up here. Squinting, he lifted his head and looked at the two men who had brought him back to consciousness.

One was Peter Hurd. The other was the bearded fisherman he remembered from his first encounter with the waterfront boss.

"You're in trouble, mister," Hurd said quickly.

"Thanks for telling me," Barney said.

"Getting flip won't help you none. I understand you've been following me

276

around for the last couple of hours."

"So what?" Barney asked.

"You beat hell out of Carl Macklin. He called me as soon as he came to. He says he didn't say a word to you, but that yellow little rat was lying, wasn't he?"

"Maybe," Barney said.

"What did he tell you?"

"Enough," Barney said.

Hurd laughed. "You think you're tough, mister?"

"Tough enough," Barney said.

"Like I said, you're in trouble." Hurd stood with his thick legs spread wide apart as if balancing himself on a restless deck. Barney was assailed with a sudden fear and he listened for the sound of a Diesel motor that would indicate that the dragger had been taken out to sea. He heard nothing and sighed with relief. They were still moored to the dock. Hurd looked down at him as he lifted himself and sat on the edge of a bunk. The man's face was stony, hard and cruel. "Worse trouble than you think, Hammond. If I called the cops now, they'd lock you up and throw away the key."

"Go call them," Barney said. "Right now."

"You wouldn't want that," Hurd grinned. "They're looking for you on a murder charge."

"I didn't kill anybody."

"You'd have a hard time convincing the cops about that. Petersen got hold of your fight manager, that little slicker named Santini. Santini's a little sore at you, mister. He claims you stole three thousand dollars from him after your fight with Reagan and he says he heard you say you'd kill Lil Ollander. He says he left you alone, sleeping in the hotel room in Boston, for over three hours yesterday afternoon. Petersen thinks you came back to Easterly and stuck that harpoon through the girl."

"To hell with Petersen," Barney said.

"You still want to see him?"

"Go get him," Barney said.

Hurd didn't move. He slicked a quick glance at the bearded silent fisherman behind him and the other man grinned and chuckled but didn't say anything. Barney reached in his pocket for his wallet. It wasn't there.

"Give me my money back," he told Hurd. "Three thousand clams."

"It ain't yours," Hurd said. "You stole it."

"It's mine," Barney said. "Give it back."

Hurd sighed. "I'm trying to be reasonable. You've caused me a lot of trouble, mister. Nothing that can't be straightened out, but you've been a nuisance just the same and I'd like to square accounts with you. You're not going anywhere. You're not leaving here. And I'm not calling the cops until I'm ready for it. You're going to stay here until you decide to cooperate."

Barney was surprised. "Cooperate?"

"We can make a deal. You understand me? You get your dough back to help your brother out with his schooner and maybe a grand or two extra as a bonus. All you've got to do is tell me what you did with the box."

"What box?" Barney asked.

"Pedro's cash box," Hurd said quietly.

Barney laughed. "I don't have it."

"I think you do."

"You're wrong," Barney said. "I wish

279

I did. I wish I knew where it was myself."

"You know what was in it?"

Barney wished his head would stop throbbing. He was in no condition for this kind of verbal fencing. He had the feeling that he was treading on thin ice or balancing on a tightrope over a fatal depth and if he made any kind of a slip, he would plunge down to certain death. Death was in Hurd's pale, cold eyes, in the calm assurance of the other man's voice. He looked from Hurd to the bearded fisherman.

"I need a drink," he said.

"After you tell me what I want to know."

"I feel sick," Barney said.

"You'll feel a lot worse if you don't answer me."

Barney pulled himself up from the bunk. His knees turned rubbery and he started to fall and Hurd caught him and slammed him back into the bunk. The man's voice shook with repressed anger.

"Answer me!"

"To hell with you!"

"Where is Pedro's box?" Hurd shouted.

Barney suggested where he might look for it, using a neat choice of four-letter words. He stood up again. Hurd nodded to the bearded man, who stepped forward and suddenly grabbed Barney's left arm and twisted quickly. Barney slammed back against the supporting post of the bunk and slid to the deck. Pain nauseated him. The blackness came back in quiet folds. He felt a foot slog into his ribs and he looked up at the dim, grinning face of the bearded fisherman.

From a great distance he heard Peter Hurd's voice.

"Maria said she gave the box to you."

"What?"

"You heard me. Where is it?"

"To hell with you," Barney said again.

The bearded man really went to work on him then. The rest was a nightmare.

17

TIME was a slow river of pain that moved sluggishly down a long bloody channel, taking him through it with light and dark, silence and sound. Afterward he did not remember all the details. Hatred consumed him. He lived on it, fed on it as it devoured him in turn and helped him survive. When he looked up at Hurd's big, blocky body and adamant face, he knew what blood lust meant, what a man tried to express when he insisted he had to kill. He wanted to kill Peter Hurd. He knew he would, some day, somewhere, he would even the score, if he lived.

There were times when he wanted to die, when he wished for a black oblivion to end the torment of questions and bodily pain. He knew that he screamed with his hatred and his pain, but no one came to help him. He was alone in a dark pit in the bottom of the vessel and there was nobody to hear him.

The questions were endless.

"You think it was Durand?" Hurd asked.

"I know it was."

"Can you prove it?"

"Yes," Barney said.

"You were up in Osterport, weren't you?"

"Yes."

"You talked to Bryson Jay?"

"Yes."

"But *you* killed the girl."

"No."

He lay on the bunk, suspended in a personal hell of his own, aware of a creeping cold that seemed to suck the marrow from his bones. There was no part of him that did not pulse with a slow and deadly pain. He was hungry and thirsty, but he fed on his thoughts of hate.

"The box," said Hurd. "Where is it?"

"I don't know."

"But you know what was in it?"

"I can guess."

"Tell me."

Barney spit in the face that bent over him, then ducked his head aside to avoid the inevitable blow. Afterward, he thought he slept. He wasn't sure. His mind floated free, remarkably light and clear, surveying the past and everything in it, examining each facet of the happenings that had beset him since his return to Easterly. It was all very simple. If he survived, he could clear it up easily. Bloody simple. And it all made sense. Fear bred panic and panic the rage of a cornered rat and a killing lust that could only slake its thirst with blood He dreamed of Lil, of her half-naked body offered to him, of her mocking laughter when he reached to hold her. Money showered down around her, green currency that tangled in her hair and slithered over her round, smooth flesh to cascade in a heap at her feet. He tried to pick up the money with a pointed stick that became a harpoon and instead of spearing the money he was standing over Lil, watching the terror in her face as he thrust the barb deep into her velvet body.

He awoke shivering, numb with cold. He was alone.

His body was paralyzed. He couldn't move. There was no light anywhere, nothing but a smothering cold darkness that seemed to vibrate with its emptiness. He wondered if death was like this. When he tried to raise his arms, however, he felt the quick bite of harsh cords on his wrists, and they made him feel better. He was alive, his senses were still working. Summoning his strength, he tried to figure out where he was and guessed he was in the ice hold of the *Lucky Q*. There was no way of telling the time. He had the impression that a number of hours had passed, perhaps a full day, but he couldn't be sure.

He relaxed against the cords, felt them give a little. He was in a sitting position on the rough and splintery deck, his back against a bulkhead. Hunger gnawed at his belly and thirst made his throat like sandpaper. Maybe they were going to starve him into talking. When he thought of Hurd and his bearded muscleman, his hatred gave him new impetus and he began to work slowly at the ropes that held him.

Perhaps an hour went by before he heard the voice calling his name.

The voice was soft and careful. He did

not recognize it. A light flickered briefly overhead and was gone. He wondered if it was a trick of some kind. Footsteps moved above him then came down a ladder nearby. He tried to call out and a croaking sound came from his dry throat and the noise he made frightened him. He tried it again.

"Barney?" The voice came back to him. "That you?"

"Over here," he managed to say.

More cautious movements in the darkness surrounding him. The light flickered again, vanished, came back and remained on, shining in quick, darting movements over the rough bulkheads of the icepen. He thought he heard Jo's voice whispering something, but he knew that couldn't be. Maybe he was dreaming all this. Nobody knew where he was. Nobody would come to help him anyway. He had been alone for so long, he had given up hope of anyone coming here for him.

The light shone in his face, blinding him. He couldn't see beyond the glare. He heard someone gasp and a man muttered something, cursing in dull anger and then Jo held him, her hands trembling, her face pressed against his. He couldn't understand her quick, murmured words. A knife gleamed briefly in the glow of the flashlight and he felt the cords fall away from his wrists and ankles.

"Jo?" he whispered. "Is that you?"

"It's all right. Let me help you to your feet," she said quickly.

"Who's with you?"

"Me," said the man. "Fred Alvarez."

"The cop?"

"I'm not acting as a cop right now, Barney."

"Good," Barney said.

Jo said: "What did they do to you? Barney, what did they want? Was it Hurd?"

He answered only her last question. "It was Hurd."

"Come on," said Alvarez. "We haven't much time."

The cop's arms held him up. His legs refused to function and he sweated and fought the numbed nerves and muscles of his body. Jo helped support him on his other side. She was talking, saying something to him, but he didn't listen.

Finally he got his legs into some sort of response. But he couldn't get up the ladder. He told himself it was impossible. He could never make it. He put one foot up on the lowest rung and felt Alvarez struggle with his weight, boosting him up. He could have wept with anger and frustration. It was childish, ridiculous. Finally he pulled himself up on the first rung. Then the next. Jo's voice kept talking to him, giving him almost tangible strength. The hatch overhead was open. Cold air touched his face, a breeze that smelled of the tangy salt harbor filled his lungs.

He rested on the deck for a moment. It was night. The fog was gone.

"How long have I been here?" he asked Jo.

She told him. It had been almost twenty-four hours. It was the next night.

He wasn't sure of what happened immediately afterward. He remembered riding in a car and Jo brought him some food, hot coffee that he drank endlessly, hamburgers and brandy. He ate in the car while Fred Alvarez drove. He had the impression that they were driving aimlessly through Easterly, up one street and down another, while Jo and the little cop considered what to do with him. Between cups of coffee, he asked how they had found him. It had been a slow process of elimination until Fred Alvarez spoke to his brother Sol, the former owner of the *Lucky Q.*, and the fisherman had mentioned Barney's previous attempt to board the dragger. The cop then trailed Hurd and the bearded man, whose name was Sykes, to the *Lucky Q.* early that evening and waited until the waterfront boss and his henchman left before they searched the dragger and found him.

The food revived Barney somewhat. The brandy and coffee brought back some of his strength. He would probably have been a hospital case, he thought wryly, if he hadn't been in training for his fight with Reagan. Jo thought he belonged in a doctor's hands, anyway. She said so, urging him to let her drive him to the Easterly hospital. He refused. He told her he was all right. Then he kissed her.

"I'm sorry, Jo."

"There's nothing to be sorry about."

"It isn't over yet," he said.

"I know."

"But I'm going to finish it tonight."

"Do you know who killed that girl?"

"Yes," he said.

"And the DeFalgia brothers?"

"Yes."

Her voice was quiet. "I see."

She didn't say any more. She understood what he had to do. He searched his pockets. The gun he had taken from Petersen's cop and the wallet with Santini's three thousand dollars in it were gone. Hurd had them. He stared at the back of Fred Alvarez' head as the man drove Jo's car through the dark streets. They went by the Town Hall and he saw the clock in the tall tower that lifted over the town and acted as a beacon for vessels entering Easterly Harbor. It was only ten o'clock.

"Fred," he said. "Are we going to drive around all night?"

"I'm trying to figure out what to do with you," the cop said. "If one of Petersen's boys stops us, our goose is cooked. If Hurd catches up with us, we're in just as bad shape. Maybe Jo is right, though. Maybe you ought to get yourself to a doctor and rest for tonight."

"I wouldn't get any rest," Barney said. "Petersen would show up right away."

"Maybe if we told the doctor — "

"It would only get whoever we picked into trouble," Barney said. "And I won't let you or Jo stick your necks out any more for me. It isn't that I'm not grateful. But I'm feeling better now. I'm all right."

"You should be hospitalized for a week," Jo said.

"I'll rest later. When it's all finished."

"Can you finish it?" she asked quietly.

"I'm going to try." He told Fred Alvarez to drive up Portugee Hill to the widow's house. "I want to talk to Maria Rodriguez. Alone."

"Petersen's already talked to her," the cop protested. "That won't buy you anything."

"Take me there," Barney said.

★ ★ ★

The cottage was dark. He asked Alvarez and Jo to stay in the car, parked a half block down from the widow's house and then walked slowly along the bleak, deserted sidewalk to the front door. Nobody was in sight. The brandy and the food had worked a minor miracle. He was aware of stiffness and pain all through him, but Hurd and his men hadn't broken any ribs or effected any serious damage. And he told himself that he was almost at the end of all this. The knowledge that he was almost finished with the whole thing gave him fresh strength and after he rang the bell he looked back at the parked car where the cop and Jo waited. He felt sorry for Jo, but nothing could be done about it. What else could he do? In the long run everything would work out for the best. He was sure of it.

Nobody answered the bell. He tried the door and found it was unlocked. He paused, considering it for a moment, then shrugged and pushed it inward, stepping into the warm, dark hallway. The living room was to the right, familiar from his last visit here over a week ago when he had caught Mal Durand with the widow. The room was empty now, dimly lighted by the glow of the street lamp that filtered through the window. He listened, but there was no sound in the house. A car went by on the street outside, but it didn't slow down or stop. He walked on down the hallway into the kitchen where he had last seen the handsome brunette widow. The kitchen shone spotlessly clean and tidy.

He felt a curious reluctance about going upstairs to the bedrooms, but it had to be done. The upper hallway was patterned with flowered wallpaper, similar to the two bedrooms up here. He went into the largest one first, facing the street. It was empty. He looked in the closet and in the light from the window he saw two suitcases and hauling them out he opened them on the chenille bedspread. The leather suitcase was heavy and fully packed with new clothing. In a small oilskin pouch in one of the inner pockets of the smaller suitcase he found a thick packet of currency, held together by an initialed money clip. He went to the window to examine the currency in the light from the street lamp. There was three thousand dollars in crisp new bills. The gold clip was Lil's. It was one that he'd had engraved for her when they'd first met.

Barney stared at it, knew that Lil would never willingly part with either the clip or the money. How had the widow gotten the money from Lil? Was it before or after Lil had been murdered? Thoughtfully, he replaced the money and oilskin pouch back in the suitcase and put them in the closet. The widow had been planning to go somewhere, but she hadn't left yet. He walked back into the second bedroom at the rear of the house.

He stood in the doorway and thought: *She'll never go anywhere again.*

Whatever gamble the widow had been making, she had lost. The price she paid was too high.

The back room had been used as a sewing room, with only a small cot against the sloping attic wall. A sewing machine stood near the window and the tiny light fixed over the needle still shone over the cloth spread on the dropleaf — a faint light that had been invisible from the street but showed up every detail of the ugly scene. Maria Rodriquez sat slumped over the machine. She was dead. A dark red stain spread across her back from the knife that was thrust into her body up to the hilt.

Barney shuddered. Sickness and anger churned inside him. The killer liked to use knives and he was expert with them. The widow had never had a chance to know what was happening to her.

After a moment he crossed the room and stood on the other side of the machine, looking down at the dead woman's face. His anger grew. Then he saw the black enameled cash box at her feet. A familiar box, taking him back to his own childhood days. It was Pedro DeFalgia's. He was not surprised to see it there on the floor beside the dead woman. When he knelt and picked it up, he was not surprised either to find it empty.

He felt a twist of pity for Maria. He knew very little about the widow but enough to let him figure it out for himself without much effort. She had played for what she could get out of it and all it had bought her had been hope first, then terror, and finally death. Maybe she had been genuinely fond of old Pedro DeFalgia; maybe she had actually intended to try to be a good wife to him. It was over and done with. When she heard Pedro was lost at sea, she had taken the chance to salvage something from her lost efforts. She had gone to the DeFalgia house and taken old Pedro's tin cash box for the papers that were in it — papers that could hang some one, papers that contained deadly knowledge to one man in this town — a little piece of paper, perhaps, but on it was the evidence that would lead to open disgrace and ruin.

The dead woman had gambled and lost in her attempt to gather birds for what she had stolen. She must have gone to Hurd and maybe even Chief Petersen with what she had, trying for the highest price. But she went to one man too many and her payment was the knife in her back.

Barney let out his breath in a long,

exhausted sigh. The house was as quiet as it had been before. He left the little light on over the sewing machine and returned to the front bedroom and from the window he saw that Jo's car was still there, waiting for him down the street.

What he had to do was best done alone, he thought.

He left the house by the back way, quickly and silently.

18

A PROWL car nosed around the corner and eased down the street, moving slowly with just the dimmers lit. Barney waited in the shadows and watched it go by. The night was clear and cold, the wheeling sky swinging into October. From the church tower nearby came the solemn bells ringing out the hour. It was just eleven o'clock. He shivered a little and worked his arms in his coat, loosening the stiff and bruised muscles. His hatred was a fire that warmed his belly, gave him strength. What he was doing was for himself, first of all, he thought, and only in the interests of justice as a secondary factor. The murderer was a personal symbol now, an object for vengeance, for evening the score. He had to do it alone. He didn't know what Jo would be thinking of now, waiting for him on that dark street across from the widow's house. Maybe Fred Alvarez had already followed him into the house to look for him and had found the dead woman. It didn't matter. Maria had been dead for many hours to judge by the way she looked and the cop would know he'd had nothing to do with it. Jo would guess why he had left without returning to the car though and it was only a matter of time until she anticipated this next move and tried to stop him.

But nothing was going to stop him now, he told himself.

The prowl car turned the next corner and was gone. Barney quit the shadows under the trees and walked across the lawn toward the big stone house. He went in by the back way, through the shedlike summer kitchen and across the wide, tiled kitchen floor with its corner fireplace and down the wide hallway to the front room. A light shone beyond the folding library doors and a fire crackled in the big Vermont fireplace in there.

Malcolm Durand sat at a desk, his dark head bent over a ledger. He wore wide-bowed reading glasses and smoked a pipe thoughtfully as he worked. He didn't hear Barney's entrance. Barney paused quietly, listening for any other sound of occupancy in the house. He heard nothing. He knew Durand had a housekeeper and gardener, but there was no sign of them. Perhaps this was their night off or they had gone to the local movies. It was better this way, he told himself. Better to do it alone.

"Durand," he said quietly.

Durand's head came up, but for a moment he didn't turn around to face Barney. He was wearing a red smoking jacket and Moroccan leather slippers on his small feet. His shoulders moved, as if a shudder touched his body. The fire crackled comfortably on the hearth. The room was big, luxurious, undoubtedly one of the finest and most expensively furnished rooms in Easterly, Barney thought. He smiled wryly. He watched Durand's hand edge toward the telephone and he said briefly: "Don't."

The hand stopped moving and Durand turned around in the chair and started to stand up then sank back again.

"Surprised?" Barney asked.

"Where did you come from?"

"Out of that little private hell you

arranged for me," Barney said.

"You're a fool," Durand said. "Where have you been hiding for the past twenty-four hours? The police have a state-wide alarm out for you. No matter where you try to hide, Hammond, you'll be caught."

"I haven't been hiding. You know that."

"I don't understand," Durand frowned. He started to rise again.

"Sit down," Barney said.

"I'm going to call the police."

"Sit down!"

Durand made a swallowing sound in his throat. But he was not afraid. There was no sign of fear in the man's handsome face. He touched his thin, dark mustache and for an instant Barney's mind spun backward to his school days, to the old, old rivalry between himself and this man who was now the richest and most powerful figure in Easterly. He remembered old fist fights in the schoolyard, the frenzy of the unreasonable grudge that lived like a wall between them. Senseless, up until now. Now was different.

"Mal, we haven't much time," he said quietly. "Don't pretend not to know where I've been or what happened to me. Your man, Hurd, did his best to make me tell him what I know. But he didn't learn anything from me. It was the other way around. He made a slip of the tongue and he put the whole thing together for me with the clincher. Let's not pretend any more."

Durand said: "I still don't know what you're talking about. I haven't seen or spoken to Peter Hurd for two days."

"You're lying."

Durand's jaw came forward angrily. His eyes looked hot. "Look here. In five minutes I'm going to call the police. Five minutes. That's all the time you have to get whatever fool notions you have out of your head. I know what you're thinking. And I'll give you my answer right now, in one word. No. I didn't kill anybody. I haven't had anything to do with the murders. You've followed me and you've dug around and you've got a lot of crazy ideas that you think might make me fit the pictures in your mind, but you're wrong. I'll repeat what

I've said. I didn't kill anybody."

Barney said: "Not even Maria?"

Durand stared at him. He looked confused. "The widow?"

"She's dead. Knifed. I just left her house."

"You — "

Barney shook his head. "I found her that way. I can prove *I* didn't do it, because your errand boy, Peter Hurd, had me down in the ice box of the *Lucky Q.* since last night, playing nutcracker with my head and ribs. A cop got me out of there. A cop and your wife. This is one cop who doesn't worry about whether he keeps his job with Petersen or not. He hates Petersen's guts and he hates the way things are run in this town — the way *you* run things in this town. He and Jo got me free about two hours ago and they were with me when I went into Maria's house."

"Jo?"

"She won't say anything against you," Barney said. "She's too loyal for that. She takes her marriage vows seriously. But she's in love with me and always has been and I'm in love with her. When this is all over, I'm going to have her."

His taunt was deliberate, trying to goad the man out of his self-possession. It didn't work. Durand looked at him and rubbed his little mustache and smiled, a gesture that was just a quirk of the tiny muscles around the corners of his hard mouth.

"I've known about you and Jo for some time," he said quietly. "I guess I've known how she loved you since before we were married. All I had was the hope that you would never come back to Easterly."

"But I did come back," Barney said bluntly. "And I've upset your cute little apple cart in more ways than one."

"Yes, you have."

"And I'm going to finish you in this town. Tonight. Now. I'll agree to your five-minute ultimatum. At the end of that time we're going to call the police. You can even call Petersen personally. It doesn't matter. Because you're calling the press at the same time and Petersen won't be able to shut me up or keep me quiet about what I know about you."

Mal Durand said: "And just what is

it you think you know?"

"You killed Pedro DeFalgia," Barney said.

"You're insane!"

"You'd like to think so. But it all adds up. You've been trying to cover your tracks ever since it happened, going crazy with it and making your errand boy, Peter Hurd, run his legs off. But I've got the truth of it anyway."

"I was in Boston that day!"

"You were on the *Lucky Q.*," Barney said. "And the *Lucky Q.* is the dragger that rammed my brother's dragging gear. It won't be difficult to prove that she was the boat that came out of the fog that day. There's new paint on her bow and the only reason nothing was done about it until now is that I wasn't sure what the whole thing meant. Not all of the pieces fitted together until I saw Jo unpacking your sea-going togs last night. And then I was tipped off about a man named Bryson Jay up in Osterport. He's the wharf superintendent up there and a little pressure will crack him like a dried-out nut. He knows the *Lucky Q.* put in at Osterport on the day Pedro was killed, the day of the fog. And there was only one reason why that dragger touched port so soon. It was to put you ashore so you could return to Easterly by train, as if you had just come back from Boston. It won't be hard to check in Boston either and show that you never attended any banking conference there."

Durand sat down at the desk. His face was pale. Barney watched his hands rubbing his knees. The fire on the hearth made a quick, snapping noise.

"Don't try for a gun, Mal," Barney said.

Durand looked up at him. "Are you armed?"

"Time's running out, Mal," he said. "Do you deny that you were on Hurd's dragger?"

"No," Durand said heavily. "I don't deny it."

"Old Pedro DeFalgia had the goods on you, didn't he?"

"Yes. The old man had quite a few affidavits."

"He could prove that you and Peter Hurd had entered into a criminal conspiracy to control the waterfront and the local fishing industry by terror and violence, couldn't he? He went from one former fishing captain to the other, getting their stories about how you and Hurd squeezed them out of business by threat, by framing accidents, by lowering prices for their fares at the cannery, refusing them loans at the bank and God knows what other methods you used. But Pedro got enough on you to make him a target for murder. And it was one job that you wanted to take care of personally."

Durand's voice was strangely controlled and quiet. "Go on."

"All your life you've fought for power in this town. Power and money summed up everything worth living for. You wanted the biggest house in town, the power to hire and fire every man who worked for a living here. You got what you wanted — almost. And if it hadn't been for Pedro, you would have won. The old man beat you. Or threatened to, unless you killed him. Your lust for power was a substitute for your personal failures with Jo. I don't know. I don't know what makes a man like you do the things

you've done. It's happened before, all
through history, in big ways and little
ways. There've always been men like
you who want to rule in one fashion
or another. And I guess there always
will be. But you're finished. You're one
of the failures now."

"You're wasting time," Durand said
coldly. "Let's hear the rest of your
evidence."

A sudden gust of wind rattled the tall
windows of the library. A downdraft in
the fireplace sent a shower of sparks
rattling against the brass screen. Barney
drew a deep, controlled breath.

"You had to silence Pedro and you
did. You seized a lucky opportunity at
sea when you saw him in the dory, out
there in the fog, and you made the most
of it. But you weren't able to get the
other old man. Carlos managed to reach
shore knowing what had happened and
while he wasn't too bright, he was able
to figure out what you had done and he
went looking for you. At the same time,
you were prowling around the waterfront
looking for him the moment you heard
he had made it safely to land. You'd

gone to their house looking for Pedro's box of affidavits and didn't find it. You figured Carlos had it and when you met on the schooner, you outwitted the old man who was exhausted from his day's row ashore and stuck Carlos' own knife in him. You have a fine score, Mal — two old men and two helpless women.

"But you still didn't have the box. You tried to scare me off when you trailed Jo and me to the shipyard last week and took pot shots at us with the rifle. I've wondered why you didn't kill me then, when you had the chance. You've probably regretted it ever since. But all you had in mind then was to warn me off the case. You didn't succeed though and you didn't find the box. Not until the widow, Maria Rodriguez, approached you with the information that *she* had it and wanted a large chunk of dough in exchange for the papers that would ruin you and leave you open for criminal charges.

"It took Maria a week to get up enough courage to go to you and tell you she had the box. She had refused you once — the time I caught you in the widow's house. But she was frightened and wanted to get out of town and finally she approached you with it. You made a date with her tonight — after having Hurd work on me for a day, thinking *I* knew where the box was — and you paid off the woman with a knife in her back."

The wind rattled against the windows again. Durand's eyes slewed sidewise briefly to the darkness out there then returned to Barney. The man's face shone with sweat. His pale fingers drummed on the desk and he sighed.

"You can't prove any of this," he said.

"Bryson Jay up in Osterport will talk. Witnesses can be dug up to smash your Boston alibi. Somebody on the *Lucky Q.*'s crew can be made to testify."

Durand's smile was tight and false. "You're forgetting something, aren't you? You've omitted your girl, Lil Ollander. Why did I kill her, assuming your pretty theories are correct?"

"I don't know," Barney admitted.

"Maybe she stumbled onto something day before yesterday, when I went to Boston."

"I'm sure she did," Durand said. "But it's a pretty thin effort to connect her with me. I didn't know the girl. Never spoke to her and saw her only once or twice as she came and went from your brother's house. She knew nothing about me. And that's where your case collapses, Barney. I'm sorry for you. Some of what you've so ingeniously figured out is true. I won't deny my connection with Hurd. Nor will I deny going to sea that day on the *Lucky Q*. It was an act of anger that I've lived to regret. I told you how your brother Henry stormed into my bank one day asking for a loan and when I refused him, he became violently abusive and I had to throw him out. He made a number of charges then that a lot of people overheard and I lost my head in anger afterward. I wanted to see Henry smashed and finished. It wasn't enough to know that Hurd would take care of it. I wanted to see Henry ruined myself, personally, with my own eyes. I wanted that satisfaction after his insults and I took steps to be a witness when Hurd's boat overtook Henry's schooner. But I didn't shoot Pedro or kill any of the others. I've made a great effort to cover up the folly of my trip on the *Lucky Q.* You can't imagine how appalled I was when I came ashore and learned what had happened. I was frightened. I still am. I foresaw your case against me, and tried to cover up, as I said. But I didn't kill anyone, and I still don't have the papers Pedro collected against me."

Durand's voice grew stronger and more confident as he spoke. Barney leaned on the edge of the library table, aware of his own strength slipping away from him. The room felt hot, close and stifling. A momentary wave of dizziness touched him, and his vision blurred. He wondered if he had made a mistake trying to do this alone, in catering to his need for personally settling the whole mess. Maybe he should have taken Fred Alvarez along; but that would have involved Jo in this scene, and he hadn't wanted that. He told himself he was all right, and straightened up with an effort, conscious of Durand's eyes keenly watching him.

"Call the police now," Barney said. "Call Petersen."

"You really want that?"

"Call him."

"I think you should wait, Barney." Durand's voice was suddenly sober and earnest. "I'm expecting someone here at any moment. Someone whose information concerning all this should seriously affect what you're thinking."

"Who are you talking about?"

Durand shook his head. "If you'll just wait — "

"No," Barney decided. "Call the police now."

Durand hesitated, then shrugged and moved his hand reluctantly toward the telephone. But before he reached it, the instrument suddenly rang, and the sound was like an explosion in the momentarily silent room.

Durand lifted inquiring brows. "Shall I answer it?"

"Yes. Say hello. Then give the phone to me."

Again Durand hesitated, then did as Barney ordered. Barney took the telephone from him and Durand retreated

313

toward the fireplace.

Chief Petersen's voice was crackling in the receiver.

"Mal, listen. Glad I caught you at home. I've been checking on that call from old Ferris McHugh — you know, the lobsterman who lives over at Half Moon Hollow."

"Go on," Barney said.

"Well, there's a body here, all right — washed ashore some time early yesterday morning, to judge from the way the clothes dried out. It ain't pretty, Mal, but it's definitely Pedro DeFalgia."

Barney gripped the telephone tighter. He looked at Durand, as if Durand could hear what was being said. The man's face looked whiter, more strained. Excitement shook Barney's hands.

"Was he shot?" he asked.

Petersen said thicky: "He was shot, all right. The bullet's still in him, too. It's the damnedest thing, his being washed ashore like this. Like an act of judgment, I figure. It means Barney Hammond was tellin' the truth about what Carlos said before he died. There's only one thing funny about it."

"What's that?" Barney asked.

"Pedro was shot in the back."

"In the back?" Barney whispered.

"That's right."

Barney listened to the chief's voice go on, describing the details of the body's discovery, but he didn't hear the words. He stared at Mal Durand across the room. He felt the pound of blood all through his body and the room blurred before his eyes. He rubbed a hand over his face and heard the cop's voice go on in the receiver.

"Do you get it, Mal?" Petersen was asking. "You know what it means? Mal, are you still there?"

"This is Barney Hammond," Barney said quietly. "I'm at Mal Durand's house. Come over here."

"What?"

Barney hung up.

19

HE wasn't prepared for Durand's next move. Terror was stamped on the man's face, a misunderstanding of what had been said to Barney over the telephone. He made a thick sound in his throat and swung away from the fireplace, heading for the door. Barney's reaction was too slow to stop him. He yelled to Durand to wait, to listen to what he had to say, but the man paid no attention. Then he lunged after him.

Durand was in the hallway, running for the back of the house. Barney shouted again, but the man didn't hear his words through the panic that gripped him. He was across the kitchen yanking open the back door before Barney reached the opposite door.

"Mal! Come back here!"

The rising wind buffeted into the room in a breath of cold, bitter air. Durand looked back over his shoulder and his face was distorted queerly by the fear in him. Barney cursed his own vagueness and plunged out into the night after him. The wind made moving shadows all around him and for a moment he lost sight of Durand's running figure. Barney stumbled down the back steps and paused, weaving on his feet. He felt as though he were swimming through some obscene nightmare. He couldn't give chase to the man. There was no strength left in him. He stumbled forward, fell to one knee, picked himself up and ran on again.

"Mal!"

Movement stirred the shadows in the driveway and he turned that way, glimpsing Durand's crouching figure. Someone else was there, another shadow that rose up out of the gloom of the shrubbery directly in front of the fleeing man. There was a glint of metal, the flash of flame, the quick, flat report of a gun. Durand's scream of protest was cut off in mid-voice. He ran on for two more steps, a puppet-like figure with arms spread wide, trying to balance himself. Then his legs went as if cut out from under him and he hit the graveled driveway on both knees, skidded on his face and lay still, sprawled in the windy darkness.

Barney ran as if forging his way through some thick, viscous liquid that made everything seem slowed up, agonizingly unreal. He looked for the other man, the skulker in the shrubbery, but he didn't see anyone. The killer had vanished as quickly as he had come, swallowed up in the dark wind. The wind was all around them, roaring in Barney's ears, shaking the world as he knelt beside Mal Durand.

Durand was dead. He had been shot point-blank in the face and there was little left of his head except a welter of splintered bone and flesh and his eyes, glaring with fear and hatred, reflecting the burnished, windswept starlight overhead. One of his leather slippers had come off and his velvet smoking jacket was hunched up over his shoulders. Blood made a quickly spreading, dark stain on the gravel of the driveway.

Barney didn't touch him. He tried to get up and couldn't. The roaring in his ears grew louder. He wondered if he was going to pass out, but the sickness saved him. For several minutes he was lost in the nausea that gripped him, the violent illness that shook his body. He had never wanted Mal Durand to end like this. It wasn't right. It didn't fit with everything he had figured out. It was senseless, without rhyme or reason. What was it Mal had said? *I'm sorry for you, Barney. Sorry for you, sorry for you.* He should have listened, but he had been gorged with his own hate, his own sense of final triumph, too intent on this last bitter victory over the man who had been his rival since school days.

He lifted his head and looked down the driveway toward the street. Nobody was there. Nobody seemed to have noticed the quick shot that had ended Mal Durand's flight. The surrounding houses were dark and quiet. There was only the sudden wind that seemed to have come from nowhere, scouring the sea and the land, shaking the trees overhead.

He looked down at the dead man and wondered what had been in Mal Durand's mind in those last moments of panic-stricken flight. Guilt? Shame?

Remorse? To lose his position of respect and authority in this town would have been worse than this sudden death that had overtaken him. No matter what else had happened, Durand had lost everything, seen it all go glimmering away in Barney's words back there in the comfortable, expensive house he had built on Orient Street. It was a fishermen's town and anyone who betrayed them would be hissed and spit at on the street. Life would have been intolerable for Mal Durand when the truth of his conspiracy with Peter Hurd came out. Maybe that was what Durand had been running from when he burst out of the house. Barney wondered and then stopped thinking about it. It didn't matter now. It was over. He had been following a blind trail, spurred by a distorted emotion that had come back like a boomerang to crush him. He had been wrong about Mal, thinking he was the killer. The killer was still loose somewhere with a gun in his hand, moving through the windy night, hiding in the darkness. A man with blood on his hands and a crazy theory in his twisted mind.

Vaguely he remembered that Durand had been expecting somebody at his house, somebody involved in the murders. That person must have been hiding outside; he had taken advantage of Durand's headlong panic and killed him.

Footsteps grated on the street beyond the driveway. Barney stood up. His legs trembled. He turned to face the two men who came running up the driveway toward him.

The first was his brother Henry, tall and spare, without a hat or coat, his unruly yellow hair blowing forward in the wind. The second man was Gus Santini.

Barney wavered toward them, his mind questioning their presence. Henry caught him as he started to fall again.

"Barnabas, for God's sake, what happened here? Mr. Santini and I heard a shot and we looked up and down the street — " Henry paused and stared at the dead man behind Barney. "Is that Mal?"

"It was," Barney said dully. "Was he expecting you over here tonight, Henry?"

"Of course not. Is he dead? Barnabas, you didn't — "

"No, Henry." Distantly, from the lower part of town, came the wail of a siren. Barney felt Henry's strong, thin hands tighten around him. He said: "That will be Chief Petersen. I just spoke to him over the phone. They've found Pedro's body. It was washed ashore some time yesterday morning. I told Petersen to come over here."

"Was this before that shot I heard?"

Barney nodded. "Yes, before Mal was killed. He was expecting someone and he told me to wait before calling the cops, but I didn't."

"Barnabas, the police mustn't find you like this! Petersen will blame you for everything!"

"I suppose so," Barney said.

"Well, don't you care? Don't you want to do anything about it?" Henry's voice was angry, harsh. "Are you just going to stand here and let them take you?"

"I'm tired," Barney said. He looked at Gus Santini. "What brought you here?"

Santini looked unsure of himself. "I just arrived. Thought maybe I could help you, Barney. I still hold your fighting contract. But I didn't know you were in so much trouble. Henry told me you were hiding from the police. Got to thinking it over — that fat cop tricked me into spoiling your alibi. I know you didn't kill Lil, Barney. Listen, kid, I've done a lot of bad things to you, but I sure wouldn't frame you. Guess you know, Lil was never really your girl. She was mine. I'm sorry about the whole thing, Barney. I never wanted you to get caught in a murder rap. That afternoon in Boston, when I left you asleep in the hotel I was gone a couple of hours. I had to tell the cops the truth, didn't I?"

"Thanks," Barney whispered. "Thanks for nothing."

The sirens were much nearer now, but he didn't hear them.

Henry said: "Look here, we can get away on the *Mary Hammond*. She's in the river now, ready to sail. I had the shipyard rush the repairs and she was launched yesterday. I can sail you to Canada — "

Barney wasn't listening. He looked at Gus Santini's face and he thought of what Gus had said and a last spark of anger gave him strength to swing in a looping right at his fight manager's jaw. The blow was wild and the effort threw him off balance, out of Henry's grip. He went spinning away after it, falling away into a twisting darkness, followed by his brother's harsh cry. He thought he felt Henry's hands on his shoulders, picking him up again, but he thought: *Let me go. Let it all go.* And he let himself sink into the dark exhaustion that waited for him.

20

THE earth rocked and heaved and plunged under him in a twisting, erratic action that brought him swimming up from the dark where he had been dreaming. The motion was familiar, something out of his lost years and he frowned in his half-sleep, trying to remember what it was. He ought to remember, Barney told himself. He seemed to hear the crash and reverberation of angry seas and then a particularly violent motion under him threw his arm against something hard and unyielding and drove pain up into his mind, bringing him fully awake.

"Hello, Barney," Jo said.

He looked up at her face, smiling down at him. He didn't believe it. She had no right to be here, he thought. She's Mal Durand's wife. Then he remembered — Mal was dead. Alarm touched him, brought him fully to the present and he raised up on one elbow.

"Jo?"

"You've slept through the whole day and night," she said quietly. "It's morning again."

She was wearing an old oilskin slicker, much too large for her and a dripping wet sou'wester was pushed back on her head, exposing the soft shine of her burnished honey-colored hair. She looked tired. There were violet smudges under her eyes and tiny lines of strain around her soft mouth that had no right to be there. He looked beyond her and discovered that he was lying on a wide bunk. He was in the skipper's cabin of the *Mary Hammond*. It was a broad cabin, well toward the stern, preserved as it had been a generation ago when the schooner fished for cod off the Grand Banks using dories and a spread of white sail. When the *Mary Hammond* had been converted into a Diesel-powered dragger, it had been Henry's whim to preserve the cabin just as it had been in their father's day.

Everything came back to Barney in a rush.

"Where is Henry?"

"Up on deck, at the wheel. We've been

riding out a storm ever since the night we left."

"We're at sea?"

"Of course," Jo said.

He sat up warily, sliding his long legs over the edge of the bunk. He stared at Jo's pale face. "But the crew?"

"Henry rounded up a half dozen oldtimers just before we got away."

"And you came, too."

"I wanted to," she said simply.

"But why? How did you happen to be where you could come aboard?"

"I wanted to be with you, Barney. I thought of the schooner and got rid of Fred Alvarez after you didn't show up and Fred found Maria Rodriguez' body. I hunted everywhere for you then thought of the schooner. I went down to the river just in time. Henry didn't want me to come along, but I insisted."

Barney stared at her again. "Then you know about Mal?"

She nodded silently.

"I didn't kill him," Barney said.

"I know that."

Her eyes were sober. Barney felt the sea crash over the deck above. The schooner was making heavy weather of it. He said: "Everything has collapsed on me, Jo. I'm caught in a net I made with my own hands."

"I'm sorry, Barney."

"Then you've got it figured out, too?"

"I think I've always known, darling." She flushed a little. "Are you hungry? You'd better eat something. I've got some hot soup."

"I want to see Henry. I've got to have this out with him."

"He's on deck. I don't think he's left the wheel since we cleared the harbor." Her hands pushed him back gently as he started up from the bunk. "There's plenty of time, Barney."

He drank the hot soup she brought him and afterward he slept again, not meaning to, fighting it for a few minutes while Jo watched him with solicitous eyes. It was not a deep sleep. The uneasy pitch and toss of the schooner rolled him about restlessly in the bunk. At times he heard the dim shouts of the crew and their thudding feet on the deck overhead in the intervals between seas. Once he thought Henry came below and stood over the bunk, a tall unearthly figure dripping of the violent seas, his eyes burning as he stared down at him. Barney tried to talk to him in his sleep, but the sound of the storm overrode his words and Henry shook his head and vanished. He thought it was a dream, and slept again.

When he awoke, the chronometer on the wall told him it was past noon. He was alone in the cabin. He sat up on the bunk and winced, but aside from the stiffness of multiple bruises, he was all right. The long sleep and Jo's food had served him well. He tested his legs against the roll and pitch of the laboring schooner. The sea crashed over the deck above and he heard the water run in heavy streams through the scuppers. It seemed to him that the *Mary Hammond* lacked the buoyancy she should have. She was pounding badly. He felt the heavy pulse-beat of the Diesel engine forward, heard the pistons skip for a moment, then struggle again. He went across the cabin and sat down in a chair bolted to the deck in front of the built-in captain's desk.

The desk had been his father's, removed from the clipper ship *Orient*. It was worn smooth, the mahogany lustrous with the polish of generations. He hated what he was going to do, but there was no help for it. The lamp in the overhead swung violently back and forth, casting distorted shadows of his hands as he began to examine the papers in the pigeon holes. He took his time about it. He read each one carefully, making two piles of them. When he was finished with the pigeon holes he started on the built-in drawers. They were locked, but he broke the brass catches without much effort.

He found what he was looking for after twenty minutes and put the rest of the papers aside. He watched his hands tremble as he folded those he had selected. He was at the end of the blind alley he had dreamed of and the net had fallen over him.

The door to the cabin opened then and Jo came in. She saw him at the desk and saw the papers in his hand. Her face was pale and there was a bruise on her cheekbone where the lurching of the schooner must have thrown her against something.

The violent breath of the storm came into the cabin with her. Barney helped her slam the door against the push of the wind and the rain. Her oversized slicker was streaming wet. She stumbled against him and he put his arms around her, holding her very tightly.

"Jo," he whispered.

"We're in trouble, Barney."

"I know it, honey."

"No, it's not what you think. Henry insists on maintaining his course. The schooner is taking an awful pounding. The crew is frightened, but nobody can reason with him. He's like a wild man. I think — I'm not sure Henry knows who he is."

He felt a cold chill on the nape of his neck. "What do you mean?"

"He's gone backward — in time, I mean." She was trembling in his arms. "He — he thinks he's your grandfather. On the old *Orient*."

Her teeth chattered, and he shook her. "Jo. Jo, listen to me."

"I'm afraid, Barney. It's awful!"

331

"Jo, what was Henry's original plan? When we left Easterly?"

"He said he was going to take you to Canada, where you'd be safe. He doesn't want the police to get you."

"Does he talk as if I'm the murderer?"

"Yes, Barney."

"You know that's not so."

"I know it, Barney. And right now I think he's putting on an act to frighten the crew into submission. They want to turn back, but he won't. Newfie won't guarantee how long the Diesel will hold out. He's got several leaks up forward and the pumps can just keep up with them. The storm won't be over for several hours more, according to the radio report. But Henry says the storm will help us. According to the radio, the Coast Guard has sent out a search. In this weather, nobody will find us."

The pitch of the schooner threw them together again. She was trembling violently.

"Take it easy, Jo."

"I'm frightened. I can't help it. You don't know how he is, up there at the wheel. He's yelling and singing to himself and talking to the sea. He won't let anyone near him."

"Stay here, Jo," he said.

Her hands clung to him in desperation. "No, don't go to him, Barney! Not now!"

"I've got to," he said. "He's apt to kill us all."

"Barney — "

He looked down at her.

"Barney, are you sorry I came?"

He kissed her. "No, darling. But I want you to stay here," he said again.

He left her before she could protest further. The cabin door opened on a short ladder of six steps that led to another hatchway to the deck above. White water struck at him with malignant fury when he opened the hatch and stepped out. He was not quite prepared for the violence that greeted him. Although it was just a little past noon, the sea and the sky had assumed a uniform, murky gray that made it difficult to distinguish where one element ended and the other began. The schooner shuddered and plunged, buried her bow under a giant hill of seething water and hit Barney just above the knees, tugging at him with demoniac strength. Rain stung his eyes and salt spray dashed across his face. His feet slipped out from under him and he went sliding toward the rail in a welter of roaring water. His clutching hands caught at a safety rope and held tightly to it with a strength of desperation. The sea ebbed, flowed away from him and the schooner slowly righted herself.

A shout, torn to ribbons by the scream of the wind, came to him from the pilot house nearby. A struggling figure worked its way across the forward deck and vanished down the fo'castle hatch. Barney turned toward the pilot house. Another man answered the call and before he could take two or three steps, the second fisherman had taken over the wheel at Henry's bellowed order and Henry came staggering toward him over the wet and streaming deck.

"Get below!" Henry shouted.

Henry's wet hands grabbed for him, turning him about. Rain and spray cut across his open mouth, dashing away his next words. It was impossible to talk. Another sea burst over the bow and the schooner shuddered deep inside her hull, groaning as she fought off the renewed weight of tons of water pouring over her. Henry's face was angry under the steaming sou'wester, his eyes wild.

"Get below!"

"After you! Jo will get some coffee!" Barney shouted. "I want to talk to you!"

There was no reason in his brother's eyes for a moment. His expression was as violent as the raging elements that roared around the staggering schooner. Barney glimpsed the mountainous seas, the close wall of rain that shut off all visibility. He had no idea how far from shore they were or where Henry's course had taken them since leaving Easterly Harbor. Another mountainous wave drove them both backward toward the cabin hatchway, and surprisingly, Henry yielded to the push of his hands and nodded, shouting something over his shoulder into the keening wind. The words were lost to Barney.

It seemed remarkably calm and quiet in the cabin when they tumbled inside, shutting out some of the fury on deck. Henry shook water from his hands, mopped his face and took off the sou'wester. His face was haggard and drawn, etched with deep lines of exhaustion, but his eyes burned with an inner glow that Barney had never seen there before.

"I can't stay long," Henry said. "Tom Herrick is at the wheel. He won't be able to hold her for more than a few minutes."

"Sit down, Henry. Take a rest. Where do you think we're going?"

"Why, to Canada." Henry looked at Jo, who hadn't said anything since they'd returned to the cabin. "Didn't Jo tell you?"

"We're not going to Canada," Barney said.

"But we must! The police won't give you a chance! Your only hope now is to get out of the country. This storm is a blessing in disguise. They're afraid to follow us and even if they did, they'll never find us in this mess until it's too late!"

Barney said quietly: "We're going back to Easterly, Henry."

Henry stood up. "No."

"We've got to. You'll only sink the schooner and drown us all if you stay on this course. And we can't hide anywhere from the law, Henry."

"We're not going back," Henry said.

Barney looked at Jo. The girl was huddled on the edge of the bunk. Her eyes moved from him to Henry's tall, thin figure, soft eyes that were deeply troubled.

Barney said: "Henry, does your crew know I'm aboard?"

"No. I didn't tell them anything except that we were going fishing." Henry grinned suddenly, his teeth very white against his thin, weathered face. "Jo didn't know we were going to sail either, when she came aboard looking for you." He turned and made a stiff little bow toward the girl. "I apologize, my dear, for taking you away from your dead husband."

"I would have come anyway," Jo said quietly.

"Perhaps."

"What will happen when the crew learns you're trying to get to Canada?" Barney asked.

"Nothing. These men have been with me for a good many years, Barnabas. They trust me. They've fought with me against Peter Hurd and they merely think I slipped the schooner out of the harbor to avoid interference from any of Hurd's men."

"But when they find out I'm aboard — and they know I'm wanted by the police?"

"They trust me," Henry said simply. "They'd trust me if I sailed them around the world."

"But we're not going around the world," Barney said. "We're going back to Easterly." He drew a deep breath, aware of a vast pity for this man who was his brother and yet a stranger. "It's no use, Henry. I've looked through your desk. You should have destroyed everything."

Henry smiled. "Barnabas, what are you talking about?"

"You know what I mean," Barney said. "There's one other thing, Henry. I told you Pedro's body was washed ashore. They found a bullet in him. He had been shot in the back."

"So?" Henry asked quietly.

"It makes a difference, doesn't it?"

"I don't see how."

"Don't hedge. In the back, Henry. Don't forget I was aboard that day. I saw Pedro in that dory, when the *Lucky Q.* tore up your drag gear. I remember the fog, and the way you ordered Newfie Joe to keep the horn going. It made a lot of noise, enough so that nobody could hear the shot. We all saw Pedro fall out of the dory. He'd been facing the *Lucky Q.*, shouting at them and waving them off from a collision. But he was shot in the back, Henry. You know what that means."

Jo made a little sound in her throat, but neither man looked at her. Barney's mouth felt dry. He wished he didn't have to say it. He didn't want to go on with it. He wished the seas would overcome them and send them all to the bottom, rather than let him say it.

"Henry," he said. "Pedro wasn't shot from the *Lucky Q*. He was shot by somebody aboard the *Mary Hammond*. You shot him, Henry."

Somebody sighed in the cabin. A sea washed over the deck above, thunderous in its force. Water trickled down into the cabin from under the hatch doors. Jo stood up. She started to say something then was silent. Her face was very white. Barney kept his eyes on Henry. The tall man seemed to shiver a little. His body swayed with the pitch and heave of the deck underfoot.

"You think I did it, Barnabas?" he whispered.

"I know you did it. That's why we've got to go back to Easterly. You're not running away in order to hide me from the law, Henry. You're running away to hide for yourself. You never cared much about what happened to me. You never — "

"That's not so, Barnabas."

Barney went on with it. He couldn't stop now. There was no way to retreat, no path left open except the one ahead.

"You want it to look as if I'm the fugitive running from the police. But I'm not running any more, Henry. I won't

340

let you do this to me. Once and for all, you've got to realize there's something more important than our name and the traditions of our house and family. It's all you live by, this twisted code of yours that talks to the dead past and lives in a century that's gone and buried. All your life you've tried to stop time from going on and you can't, Henry. I'm sorry for you and I don't want to tell you all this."

"Go on," Henry said harshly. "You've said too much already. Don't stop now."

"I don't intend to."

Jo said: "Barney, please, we don't have to — "

"Stay where you are, Jo. Sit down."

"Barney, can't you see — "

"Please, Jo." He kept watching Henry. "Maybe some of it is my fault. I could have stayed here and helped you with the fishing boat, lived in the house with you and worked for you. But I couldn't take the way you lived with ghosts, Henry. Your eyes were always fixed on the past, your pride was in the things our ancestors did and it's a false pride, because it reflects no merit of your own. A man has to stand on his own feet and live today, Henry. I couldn't take it and that's why I left Easterly."

"You deserted me," Henry said.

His voice was blunt and ugly. A change had come over him with Barney's words. His reproachful tone was almost childishly petulant. He stood leaning forward a little from the hips, his lank, wet hair plastered over his forehead. His eyes glistened palely in his gaunt face. Barney looked at him as if he were a stranger. He told himself that Henry was a stranger, a man he had never known and rarely understood.

He said. "I thought everything that had happened was because of Mal Durand. Everything pointed to him, it all fitted. Or almost fitted. And that was because I wanted it to fit because Mal and I hated each other for one of those instinctive reasons that makes no sense. But it went far back into the years and nothing could change it. I was sure Mal was the killer. I'd still be sure of it, if Pedro's body hadn't washed ashore — and if you hadn't gone completely haywire, Henry, and shot him when there was no reason for it.

"Now there is only one answer and it's you, Henry. You should have destroyed those incriminating papers you took from old Pedro's box. The note you signed when Pedro loaned you his life's savings to keep the *Mary Hammond* afloat. But you couldn't bring yourself to burn them nor the affidavits Pedro had collected that proved Mal Durand was engaged in a criminal conspiracy with Pete Hurd to control the Easterly waterfront."

Henry said: "You've been snooping in my desk?"

"Yes," Barney said. "I had to. I wanted to know, once and for all. I had to settle my doubts."

"And now you have no more doubts?"

"None. You killed Pedro because he wanted either his money back or this ship and you could give him neither. Normally, Pedro would have let the matter slide by, one way or another, but the widow, Maria Rodriquez, put the pressure on him and he in turn pressured you for a settlement. To pay him was impossible — not even the bank would lend you money. To lose your ship was unthinkable. You didn't know what to do. Your desperation made you turn to hate and violence. Maybe you never meant to kill him. Probably the idea never occurred to you until the last moment before you fired the shot. I'd like to think you didn't know what you were doing, really, when you killed him. It was a thing of the moment, a crazy impulse, that made you take advantage of the circumstances. The fog was right, the sound of the horn covered the report of the rifle and there was Hurd's dragger astern, a perfect pigeon for the blame. You didn't know how perfect it was then, because you didn't know Mal Durand was aboard. It worked out fine. You always were a fine rifle shot, Henry. Fog or no fog, you got Pedro just where you aimed for him.

"You were delayed when you got ashore by losing your temper over Peter Hurd and fighting with his hoodlums. It was a fatal delay, because it gave the widow, Maria, time to go to the DeFalgia cottage and find Pedro's account box. Maria always waited for Pedro at the dock and when she got the news of the lost dory she didn't waste any time. Maria was greedy. She planned to sell it to the highest bidder, but you didn't know that then. You tore the place apart, looking for that box and you didn't find it. Then you heard that Carlos, the other brother, had made his way ashore. You knew that Carlos would have a pretty good idea of what had happened and who killed his brother. You were the only one who could have taken that knife away from him though. It had to be a killing by treachery, since Carlos was murdered with his own knife. It had to be done by someone who knew him well enough to coax that knife out of his hand and use it on him the next moment. If Carlos had thought that the shot which killed his brother had come from Hurd's dragger, under Durand's orders, the murderer couldn't be Durand, because Durand could never have wheedled that knife away from Carlos. I should have figured that out earlier, but the obvious doesn't always swim right into view. Probably no one else would remember that you always clean your pipe with a knife. It was easy to borrow Carlos' knife then turn it on its owner. The obvious, but I didn't figure it then — especially when I'd fixed on another goal. I thought it was Durand and I didn't bother to think of the meaning of Carlos' death that same night."

The schooner lurched and Barney grabbed at the bunk post to steady himself. Jo sat on the bunk beside him. Henry stood near the hatchway door, swaying with the troubled movement of the vessel. His eyes were hooded, regarding Barney with hatred.

"And Lil?" Henry asked. "I suppose I killed that trollop of yours, too, eh?"

"Yes," Barney nodded. "It was one of those unfortunate things. She was running out on me with the money from my advance on the fight purse and she remained in Easterly when I went to Boston with Santini. She was in the house with you all that day. You hated her. You thought I might marry her and you didn't think she was good enough to carry the Hammond name. But that wasn't the only reason you wanted her out of the way. She was unfortunate in being in the house when you thought she was in Boston and so you told Maria Rodriguez to come to the house to talk things over. Maria must have contacted you and asked for some kind of settlement on the note she'd found in Pedro's accounts. Maybe she threatened to take it to the police as a possible motive for the murder of Carlos. She was afraid, but she was also a greedy woman and she wanted to leave town with everything she could get her hands on. You had no money and you quarreled with her. Lil overheard the conversation, didn't she? You didn't know Lil was still in the house and you spoke freely to Maria and Lil overheard every word of it. When Lil, who probably had blackmail ideas of her own, talked to you afterward, you were shocked into fury at being caught and you snatched up the nearest weapon to hand, that harpoon on the wall. You drove her upstairs and killed her in her bedroom to shut her up. That was when you found the money Lil had stolen from me."

Henry's voice was high and unnatural.

"You're guessing at this. You can't prove it."

"But it's the truth, isn't it, Henry?" Barney paused for a moment, then went on. "You took the money, the three thousand dollars, with Lil's gold clip on it, to Maria. You figured that with that amount you could buy her out for good, get the note and you'd be safe with Maria out of town. Maria had other ideas. She took the money, but she taunted you, saying she had other notes to collect on and she would leave town when she was ready. You left her house in a fury and the more you thought it over, the angrier you got. What else was in that box, you wondered. You went back later and while she was busy over her sewing, you thrust that knife in her back, didn't you, Henry? And you found the affidavits Pedro had collected to prosecute Mal Durand."

Henry said queerly: "Yes, it's all true, Barnabas. I had to kill the widow woman. She knew too much. And the three thousand dollars would have settled all my financial debts on the repairs of the schooner. I found all the papers but not the money. I never did find the money.

I took it from that girl you call Lil when she taunted me, told me how she had fleeced you again. I had to pay Maria or let her have the *Mary Hammond*. I couldn't do that. I'd sink her rather than let anyone else have her!"

"That's what you're planning to do now, isn't it?" Barney asked.

"Perhaps."

"You'd rather drown us all in some insane notion of going down in the sea in glory, rather than let the police catch up to you. It doesn't matter to you that the crew who trusts you will lose their lives, too."

"They belong with me," Henry said. "With their captain."

Jo made a small sound in her throat. Her eyes were wide, fixed on Henry's long, wavering figure. Horror grew in her look.

"And Mal?" she whispered. "Why did you kill Mal?"

Henry laughed. "I wanted to do it for a long time. After I read those affidavits I hated him more."

Barney said: "Durand knew the truth. Maybe he always knew it, from the very

349

start. And that's another thing. If the killer had been anyone else but you, Henry, he wouldn't have missed with that rifle the night Jo and I went to the shipyard. He had every chance in the world to kill us then, but he didn't. It was you and you didn't kill me because you still expected the rest of the money I'd get out of the fight purse to help you outfit the *Mary Hammond* again.

"Durand knew he wasn't the murderer and he knew it wasn't Hurd either, but he was so busy trying to cover up circumstantial evidence pointing to him due to the impulse that led him to go aboard the *Lucky Q.*, that he had no time for getting at the real murderer. But he knew Maria had the box, since she had approached him for blackmail money and he probably learned from her that you were the other blackmail victim. When I was in his library last night, he told me he was sorry for me, but I didn't know what he meant. Now I do. He knew at that moment that you were the murderer; he had known it for several hours. But he didn't want to expose you without getting back those affidavits and he telephoned you to ask you to come over and talk things out. You're the person he was waiting for last night when I was there. You agreed to talk it over with Durand, but your real aim was to kill him and silence him forever. That was your biggest mistake because, given everything else, Durand might have taken the rap for the whole business — that is, for all of it except Lil's murder. I couldn't quite tie him in with that, especially when I found the three thousand dollars with Lil's clip still fastened to the money in the widow's suitcase. Mal didn't need to murder for money and Lil would never willingly have parted with either the clip or the cash. So I couldn't figure Mal as Lil's murderer. I should have known.

"You killed Durand last night, Henry, and you used Gus Santini as an alibi. You let Gus think you were still in the house, upstairs somewhere, and you left by the back service entrance and slipped across the street to answer Durand's summons. Probably you saw me through the window talking to Durand and you hesitated to come in. Then Durand lost

351

his head and ran away from me, out of the house. Durand didn't know what Petersen had told me over the phone. He'd been living under a terrible strain for more than a week and his nerves cracked and drove him into flight. He ran right into you, Henry. You had no intention of bargaining with him for the affidavits he wanted. You couldn't let him live when he knew you were the killer. You shot him point-blank then ran back across the street and into our house by the back service stairs, went up to the second floor and ran down to the library where Gus was waiting, as if you'd never been out of the house at all. Then you came over to investigate as if you were worried by the sound of the shot."

A sudden crashing sound came from the deck above. A man's shout was snatched away by the roar of the wind and the sea. Someone's feet pounded the deck above. Henry's eyes flicked upward. He moistened his lips.

"I must get back to the wheel," he said.

Barney said: "We're going back to Easterly."

"No."

"The schooner won't live through this storm, Henry."

"I know that," Henry said and smiled.

"Henry, you can't go on with this," Barney argued.

"I must. You give me no alternative."

"I don't care for myself," Barney said. "Everything's finished for me, too. But at least, think of Jo — "

"She came along of her own free will, Barnabas."

"But she didn't know about you!"

Henry looked at the girl. "I think she knew all the time," he said quietly.

Jo stood up. Her hand slid into Barney's. Her fingers felt cool and steady. "It's all right, Barney."

"Henry, don't make me do this," Barney said tightly.

"But, my dear brother, you're not doing anything. If you're thinking of taking this vessel away from me, forget it. I won't let you. You see, I am armed."

Henry took his hand from his slicker pocket with a smooth gesture. He was holding a gun. He had been holding it on Barney all the time. His face was strange, unfamiliar. Barney's voice shook.

"You wouldn't shoot me," Barney said.

"Barney — " Jo warned.

"Jo knows better," Henry said. "Don't force me to do it, Barnabas. I didn't think it would come to this. But I can't help what I must do. I can't lose everything. If I do, I'll tear the world down with me, do you understand? We'll all go down together."

Barney looked at his brother and knew that he faced death if he moved for the gun. He wondered how he could have gone through all these years knowing so little about the man. Henry had always been older, remote from him, withdrawn into the past by his passionate pride in name and family and tradition. It was like an illness, hidden and malignant, growing in him like a cancer, blooming like a hideous flower in the dark of his own soul.

He felt sick and ugly himself, deep down inside.

A second crash came from above, louder than the first. The vessel shuddered, heeled far over to starboard and suddenly the hatch burst inward and a deluge of water poured into the cabin. Someone screamed, and the scream was drowned in the tons of raging sea that shook the schooner. Barney felt the impact of the water drive him from his feet, slamming him across the cabin. He couldn't breathe. He tried to grab for Jo and lost her. The lamp went out and the world seemed to turn over, slowly and grindingly, while from the bowels of the stricken schooner came a harsh grating sound that seemed to fill his bones. He felt himself go down and under the raging torrent of the sea.

21

HE struck something hard and unyielding and grabbed for it, clinging to it with desperate strength. It was the captain's desk, solidly fastened to the cabin floor. Barney pulled himself upright in the darkness. The water was knee-deep. He could see nothing except the faint glimmer of light from the splintered door over the hatchway.

"Jo!" he called.

The schooner groaned, righting herself slowly, but the grating noise continued. There were dim shouts from up on deck. Fear made him frantic.

"Jo!" he called again.

"I'm here," she said, speaking from the darkness.

He floundered toward the sound of her voice, stumbling over debris that floated in the dark cabin. Water gurgled in deep-throated triumph around him. A second sea came smashing down the ladder, but it was not as violent as the first. He caught Jo's arm and pressed her to him. She was trembling, but he couldn't see her face.

"Are you hurt?"

"No," she said. "Where is Henry?"

"I don't know." He raised his voice in a shout, but there was no answer. "I think he got out all right. He must be on deck. Come on, Jo."

"Barney, he isn't sane."

"I know that. Come on."

He held her hand and led her toward the glimmer of light from the hatchway. Another sea poured down on them and her fingers almost slipped away from his wet grip. He fought the demoniacal fury of the sea, dragging himself and the girl upward and out on deck.

The gray, yellowish light of the storm made the scene seem unreal, a figment of nightmare imagination. Great smoke seas raced down on them, half-burying the schooner's deck. Some of the crew struggled with debris up forward, working in panic haste. Barney looked for Henry but couldn't find him at first. The schooner lay heeled far over in the grip of the gale, laboring to right herself against the pressure of the wind and the seas. He kept a firm grip on Jo and struggled toward the pilot house. A deckhand came out, face white, eyes staring wildly. His mouth opened, but his shout to Barney and the girl was snatched away by the sound of the storm.

Barney grabbed at the man's wet slicker. "What was that?"

"Hurd!" the man yelled. "Hurd's out there in the *Lucky Q*! He just grazed us!"

Barney pushed Jo inside. "Grab hold of something, honey." Then he looked in the direction the man was pointing. Off the port quarter, the rain made dense gray sheets that wavered toward them in solid curtains of water. A dark shape smashed through the seas and the wind, keeping abreast of them. Barney couldn't mistake the chunky outline of the dragger. The deckhand had been right. He dashed rain from his eyes and scanned the damage up forward where part of the rail had been torn away. He wondered how serious the damage was below deck and watched the other dragger for a moment, trying to find reason in what was happening.

Dimly through the torrent of the storm's roar came a voice hailing them by means of a megaphone, but the words were indistinguishable. Several dark figures were visible on the dragger's deck for a moment and he thought he recognized Peter Hurd and then, with a start, fixed on the fat man beside the waterfront boss. He couldn't be sure, but he thought it was Chief Petersen.

Barney struggled with the pilot house door and slammed inside. Henry was there, at the wheel.

The sound of the storm was muted in here. Jo stood in a corner of the tiny cabin, her face pale, her shoulders squeezed against the walls. A trickle of blood came from a corner of her mouth. Barney looked at Henry. The man's eyes were wild, gloating, a part of the storm, reflecting its insane violence.

"Henry," Barney said. "Heave to. Let them board us. The police are with Hurd."

"I will not," Henry said flatly. "We're outside police jurisdiction now. They have no right to touch us."

"Heave to!" Barney repeated.

The gun seemed to grow, suddenly, in Henry's hand. "Stand back, Barnabas. Don't try to take the wheel from me. I won't let you. They're not coming aboard my vessel."

"Put that away," Barney said. "You're out of your mind, Henry. You're sick. Listen to me. You can't outrun the *Lucky Q*. That dragger out there can take this pounding all day long, but the *Mary Hammond* won't live another hour if you keep her on this course. Do you want her to go down and lose everything, after all? All they have to do is stay astern of us like this and wait for us to founder. You can't hope to get away from them before it gets dark. The schooner won't even stay afloat that long. You're playing right into Hurd's hands by making a race out of it."

Henry looked thoughtful, but the gun in his hand didn't waver. The schooner shuddered and pitched violently, but he controlled the wheel with seemingly little effort. There was the strength of madness in his tall, spare frame, the sudden scheming cunning of insane violence.

"You may be right, Barnabas. They

mustn't be allowed to laugh at me."

"Then bring her around," Barney said. "Right now."

"Yes. Yes, I will."

Rain smashed against the pilot house windows, blinding their vision. There came a sudden loud report as the storm trysail on the foremast parted with a bursting sound and the shreds of winter canvas went hurtling off on the wind, twisting and flapping away like gray ghosts, to be swallowed by the sea. Henry swung the wheel hard over and shouted into the wind to Newfie Joe, down in the engine room. For several moments the schooner failed to respond, caught in the strong grip of the wind. Then, little by little, with agonizing slowness, her head come up and she began to veer around. Barney looked aft and saw that the dragger had closed some of the distance between the two vessels. A bursting sea smashed over the broken rail forward and the struggling crew scattered like buckshot, grabbing for their lifelines. The next of dories just aft of the foremast was swept cleanly over the side as if by a giant scouring hand. A second sea broke over the bow as the schooner struggled to come into the wind. The deck creaked underfoot, tilting more and more toward the dangerous degree when she would not be able to right herself again. Henry's face was shiny with sweat. He began to shout incoherently, speaking to the schooner as if she were a live and animate thing, able to answer the cajoling and cursing he addressed to her.

Barney moved back across the pilot house to Jo. Her eyes questioned him, but he had no answer for her. He had done what he had to do; there had been no choice for him. Perhaps if he had never come back to Easterly, none of this would have happened. Jo's hand was tight in his. And if he had never come back to Easterly, he would never have found Jo again. He told himself that reproaches were useless, that there was nothing more to think about. If any of them escaped alive, there would be time enough to straighten things out with himself . . .

The schooner had come into the wind. The seas broke less violently over her bow and she rode steadier, breasting the force of the wind. Dead ahead, the other dragger rode less than a hundred yards away.

"Hold her like this," Barney suggested. "Let them come to us."

Henry didn't answer. It seemed to Barney as if the schooner were gathering speed, hurtling down on the other vessel. He heard Henry laugh as the distance closed rapidly and a glimmer of horror suddenly touched his mind as he realized what Henry planned to do. The dim hoot of a warning blast came from the other boat. One of the *Mary Hammond*'s crew came running and sliding across the deck, away from the bow. His face was stamped with quick fear. The others followed.

Barney suddenly lunged across the pilot house, grabbing for the wheel. Henry slammed the gun at him, caught him across the cheek and drove him backward.

"Stay away!"

"You're going to crash!" Barney gasped.

"Of course!"

Blood trickled warmly down Barney's cheek. They were almost upon the

363

dragger now. For a brief moment Henry's eyes flickered away toward the other vessel and Barney jumped again. He saw Henry raise the gun and heard the explosive roar as it went off in the narrow confines of the pilot house and a blaze of light blinded him. His hands closed on the wheel and he yanked at it savagely, struggling against the weight of Henry's body. The schooner heeled, started to swing. Through the rainswept windows Barney saw the *Lucky Q.* swinging in front of them, growing larger and larger —

There came a rending crash that tore through the trumpeting of the storm. His feet went out from under him and he was aware of water smashing into the pilot house, of the crazy tilt of the deck and of men screaming and shouting. He thought of Jo and fought against the drowning seas, caught at the door of the pilot house and hauled himself to his feet. Henry's shot had gone wild, but Henry was no longer in the pilot house. He looked for Jo, saw her huddled near the wheel and struggled toward her. Through the pilot house windows he saw that the schooner's bow had sliced against the copper-plated beam of the dragger. Most of the *Mary Hammond*'s crew were struggling onto the other vessel in the few moments they were locked together. He didn't waste any more time. He scooped Jo up in his arms, surprised at the soft fragility of her body. She was unconscious.

A sea swept him up and he went to his knees on the deck outside, but he didn't lose his grip on the girl. He brought up against the solid oak rail, fought up out of the scuppers to his feet again and struggled toward the other vessel. Men crowded with him, helping him over the side to the other deck. There was shouting and confusion all around him as he let someone take Jo from his arms to carry her into the dragger's deckhouse.

The *Mary Hammond* slid away and fell astern.

Someone grabbed his shoulder, spun him around on the wet and slippery deck. It was Peter Hurd. The man's face was congested with fury.

"Here he is!" Hurd shouted. "Here's the killer!"

Barney grinned tightly. "I owe you something, Pete. Now I'm going to collect."

"A pleasure," the man grated.

Hurd swung first. There was no rhyme or reason in the struggle. It was as if the madness of disaster had seized them all. Barney ducked under Hurd's big swinging fist and slammed a right into the man's belly, followed it with a left that cracked sharply on Hurd's blunt, hard face. The big man staggered back, crashed against the wall of the deckhouse and straightened, blood dribbling from his mouth, eyes hooded. Several of the crewmen started to interfere and Hurd waved them back.

"This is between me and him," Hurd panted. "Leave us be. When we clear up this mess, we'll give him the deep six with the rest of the wreckage."

The big man came forward again. Barney waited, braced against the heave and pitch of the dragger's deck. Rain drenched them. A sea burst over the rail, swirled about their legs and then Hurd lunged, trying for a grip on him. Barney slammed a left and a right against the man's head, remembering the long night he had spent in torment aboard this dragger, remembering the evils and crimes this man had committed on the waterfront. In his blows went the drive for vengeance for all those who had suffered at this man's hands. Hurd's head snapped back and he grinned, grabbed again and closed his arms around Barney in a crushing bear hug. Barney smashed his forearm at the man's blunt head and felt himself carried backward across the deck in a rush that scattered the gaping seamen. He brought up with a shock against the cabin wall. His breath was being crushed out of his lungs by the man's immense strength. Hurd had his head tucked in between his powerful shoulders, pressing against Barney's chest, pinning him to the wall. Someone shouted and tried to claw between them and Hurd shook the man aside. Barney felt his strength slip slowly away. His blows against the man's head and shoulders grew weaker. Another sea washed over them and he spun aside, felt Hurd's grip weaken and slip and they both went down, sliding with the water across the deck.

Barney broke free and scrambled to his feet. In the momentary respite, he glimpsed the *Mary Hammond* adrift astern, down by the bow, half awash in the water. Then Hurd crouched and came up at him with a rush, trying to regain his grip. Barney slid aside and put all his strength in the left that he swung almost literally from the deck. His knuckles cracked on the man's jaw and he felt bone and cartilege give way. Hurd went by him in a stumbling rush and fell flat on the deck, face down, sliding toward the rail. Barney caught at the man's legs and clung as Hurd half slipped into the sea. Someone else grabbed at the big man's body and hauled him back to safety.

Barney stood over the man. "Get up," he said. "Get up!"

Hurd's eyes were dazed. The lower part of his face was a welter of blood. He shook his head slowly and held out his hands, palm outward in a defensive gesture.

"No more," he gasped.

The craze of Barney's anger ebbed out

of him. Several of the *Lucky Q.*'s hands came forward and helped Hurd below. Barney straightened, breathing deeply, as a fat figure, slightly ludicrous in an enormous yellow oilskin coat, came forward, cautiously across the wet deck toward him. It was Chief Petersen. The cop looked baffled.

"Didn't think you could do it," Petersen said harshly. "Reckon I could've stopped your fight, but I figured you had a lickin' comin' to you — the trouble and money you cost the county tryin' to catch you. But I gotta hand it to you, Hurd's been itchin' for a lickin' a long time."

"Thanks," Barney said wryly.

Petersen said: "You got those papers Henry took from the widow woman?"

Barney looked at the man in surprise, felt inside his torn slicker and nodded. "They're wet, but maybe you can still read them."

"Whatever they are, they'll clear you and they'll break Hurd. I figure he could use a lesson or two. Guess he had an idea he could keep going even if his boss, Durand, was dead."

"I don't understand," Barney told him.

"I thought you figured me for your pigeon."

"I did," the fat cop nodded. "Until we found old Pedro's body when it washed ashore. That bullet I told you about over the phone. It came from a rifle Henry had in his house. When I saw the old man had been shot in the back, I figured the same as you did. Henry was the one I wanted."

Barney looked at the littered deck. "Where is he?"

"On the *Mary Hammond*," Petersen said quietly. "He could've jumped across with the rest of his crew when he tried to ram us, but I guess he figured his way was the best way out."

Barney looked across the seething, storm-tossed water at the derelict schooner astern. Her decks were almost awash now, her bow already under. Both masts had been torn out of her. A tall and lonely figure stood on her stern, facing the storm. It was Henry. Strangely, there was something strong and proud in his brother's posture. Then, even as Barney watched, the schooner's bow plunged all the way under, and a great sea swept up the deck toward the stern where Henry stood. The stern lifted for an instant and Henry stood facing them briefly and suddenly. As if some giant hand had reached up from below the ocean's depth, the schooner slid down, plucked out of sight.

Barney shuddered. His throat ached. He felt Petersen touch him and he saw something of his own feeling reflected in the man's eyes.

"We could've pulled him aboard with us," Petersen said quietly. "But that's the way he wanted it and I couldn't see no reason to tell a man how he should die. Henry and I went to school together, Barney. He was always kind of quiet and aloof. But whatever he done, it's over with. Even as a murderer he done this town a service. The fishermen will have a chance now. Maybe Henry tried to straighten things out the wrong way and for the wrong reasons, but he freed Easterly and the fishermen and the waterfront. I'm a free man again, too. I'll no longer have to take orders from Durand and Hurd if the people'll give me a chance again, I mean, to do a good job." He heaved a great sigh, grinned ruefully at Barney for a moment then turned and went into the deckhouse.

Barney watched the sea for a few seconds then went below to look for Jo.

★ ★ ★

The rain had stopped and the autumn storm was over. Toward the west, the setting sun broke redly through the ragged, fleeting clouds, touching the still troubled sea with warning fingers. Easterly was just over the horizon. The *Lucky Q.*, not seriously damaged by the collision, was being captained by Sol Alvarez.

The wind was cold, blowing like a clean antispetic from the north. Barney lay in the bunk wearing dry clothing loaned to him by one of the *Lucky Q*'s crew members. Petersen had brought him several cups of coffee liberally laced with rum and then had sat talking to him for a long time. Down underneath, Petersen wasn't a bad guy. The way things had been in Easterly, Petersen had had no choice but to follow Durand's orders.

Now that the waterfront mess had been cleaned up, things would be different. Barney scarcely listened to the man's quiet voice. His mind kept slipping back into the past, to his boyhood with Henry, to the big house on Orient Street that Henry had kept alive with ghosts.

"You going back to your fightin' career, boy?" Petersen asked.

"What?" Barney asked.

"I just wondered what you were going to do now."

"Hurd's got three thousand dollars of mine," Barney said.

Peterson grinned. "No, he ain't. I took it from him. He still had your wallet with all that cabbage in it. You'll find it in your clothes."

"Thanks," Barney said.

"It's enough to get started on again, ain't it?"

"Doing what?" Barney asked.

"Maybe you ought to talk that over with Jo."

"Maybe I will," Barney said.

He got out of the bunk and went up on deck. The sky was clear, cool lilac fading into evening. The sea looked as if it had been swept clean. He looked for Jo and found her up near the bow at the winches. She looked small and unhappy in her borrowed seaman's clothes. Her hair was blown by the wind. She saw him coming and smiled briefly and then kept watching the sea again as he stood beside her.

"We'll be in Easterly in an hour," Barney said.

"Yes."

"Jo, I — "

"Don't say anything now," she told him quietly. "When you come back again, after a while, things will be better."

"I'm not going away," he said.

"You're not?"

He looked at the sea and the evening sky. He kissed her. Her lips were warm and responsive.

"This is where I belong," he said. "It took me a long time to find it out, but I know it for sure now."

They stood in silence after that, side by side, watching the horizon. It was only a question of time, he thought. Time would heal everything. He would never forget, but things would be better

374

after a while. Better for him and better for Jo. He felt her hand search for his and hold it tightly.

The wind blew fair.

THE END

THE WILDERNESS WALK
Sheila Bishop

Stifling unpleasant memories of a misbegotten romance in Cleave with Lord Francis Aubrey, Lavinia goes on holiday there with her sister. The two women are thrust into a romantic intrigue involving none other than Lord Francis.

THE RELUCTANT GUEST
Rosalind Brett

Ann Calvert went to spend a month on a South African farm with Theo Borland and his sister. They both proved to be different from her first idea of them, and there was Storr Peterson — the most disturbing man she had ever met.

ONE ENCHANTED SUMMER
Anne Tedlock Brooks

A tale of mystery and romance and a girl who found both during one enchanted summer.

CLOUD OVER MALVERTON
Nancy Buckingham

Dulcie soon realises that something is seriously wrong at Malverton, and when violence strikes she is horrified to find herself under suspicion of murder.

AFTER THOUGHTS
Max Bygraves

The Cockney entertainer tells stories of his East End childhood, of his RAF days, and his post-war showbusiness successes and friendships with fellow comedians.

MOONLIGHT
AND MARCH ROSES
D. Y. Cameron

Lynn's search to trace a missing girl takes her to Spain, where she meets Clive Hendon. While untangling the situation, she untangles her emotions and decides on her own future.